## Follow Andre on Social Media

Facebook: www.facebook.com/andre.ray.18

www.facebook.com/Author.AndreRay

www.Amazon.com/author/andreray

# ACKNOWLEDGEMENTS

I would like to express my sincere appreciation to the following people without whose help this book would not be possible.

First and foremost, my Lord and Savior Jesus Christ. The Holy Spirit for inspiration in ministering this message.

I want to especially thank my lovely wife and family. Without your love and prayers to keep me going, this road couldn't be traveled. You are truly my rock in every season of my life.

Last but not least, I want to thank the readers of Christian Fiction. Without each one of you, this would not be possible. I pray that my books are a source of inspiration and hope.

# Kerry

Standing here looking into this mirror, It just hit me that I could have lost my life that night. I can still feel the barrel of James shotgun on my forehead. Those chilling words he yelled out "Get back or I'll blow her head clean off!" Still haunts me. He was so bent on getting the money out that safe. I knew I was dead until I heard Frank say, "I'm coming in, don't shoot please." After everything I've done to him, he would put his life on the line for me.

When James told me to get out and get right with my husband. I ran out bracing for the shot to the back but it never came. The grip of my husband's arms around me was like I never felt before. I couldn't even look him in the face. Why did he let me live? I still wake up with nightmares; this black dress could have been my burial outfit. I don't know why we had to have James funeral at this church.

I know he gave his life to the Lord, but I still can't forgive him. Looking into his coffin sent chills down my spine. If that wasn't bad enough, most of the men in the service out there, I been with in some fashion. My heart feels like it's coming out of my chest. Let me put some cold water on my face, can't do that because I would have to redo my makeup. I hear someone knocking at the door.

"Honey, are you ok in there?" It was my husband at the door.

"Yes sweetheart, I'll be out in a few. Please go back inside the service," I replied.

"Ok, but hurry up, we about to start the service."

Despite our age difference, I love my husband. Over the years, he has been so good to me. If anyone ever found out our secret, it would tear this church apart. I need to try and repair the damage if possible. I hate and love my lifestyle at the same time. People in this town think they know my story, good wife and first lady of the church. I wish that was the whole thing wrapped up with a bow.

Who's knocking on the door this time?

"Kerry, are you doing ok? You have been in here a long time," A male voice called out.

It was Frank, what's he doing in here.

"I just want to make sure you are fine, I know it's still a struggle for you to be here."

"A struggle!! It's a living hell! That man in that coffin, you, and all the other men I slept with in one place. Oh, you want to guess how I feel again?"

"You're right, please forgive me if you think I was belittling this event."

"What do you want Frank Mosely? You came in here to see if you can get a quickie?"

I got up on the sink counter spreading my legs; tears start to run down my face.

"I know this is what you all expect from me now so come on and get it over with!" I yelled out.

"Kerry, close your legs and get down from here, I didn't come in here for that. I saw you get up and leave out thirty minutes ago, just concern that's all. Do you want to talk about it?"

"No. I'll be alright." A smile comes over my face. "I should know by now that you're a Man of God now. Please forgive me Deacon Mosely, can I ask you something?"

"We have been friends long enough for you to ask me anything, what's your question?"

"Why did you save my life that night? I brought you nothing but pain."

"You both were worth saving that night Kerry. God's Mercy and Grace wouldn't allow you to die. I was just the tool he used that night. Pull yourself together, the world will still be on the other side of this door."

"I'll be out in a few more minutes; you do have a way with words."

"Ok, don't let me have to drag you out." We both laughed while he walked out.

I locked the door so no one else could come in. Can't stay in here forever, pull it together girl. Look at my makeup, now I have to do my face over. Good thing I packed my makeup bag, needs to put that good wife face back on for the public. As I was applying my eyeliner, I could almost see my demons staring back at me. Even in the house of God, they try my nerves. Pleaded the blood of Jesus and finished what I was doing. My life would not be this complicated if I didn't spend the night over my Cousin Kelly's house when I was ten. I can recall every ugly detail of that night. I was asleep next to my cousin when I felt a hand come over my mouth. I then was pulled out of bed by my hair, tried to break free, but I weighed only 40lbs at the time.

I attempted to bite down on his hand, that didn't work either. I could see Kelly just lying there motionless. Why didn't she wake up and help me? I gripped the frame of the door as he was prying my hands free. I didn't know who it was at the time; I just knew I was in trouble. "Please someone wake up!!" Filled my head. Little tears begin to run from my face onto his hands. I could feel them run into my mouth. Maybe this would make him stop but it didn't. He was able to get me into the bathroom located in the basement of the house. He placed me down hard on the floor. I almost blacked out from the blow to the back of my head.

Before taking his hand away from my mouth, he put his face so close I could smell his funky breath. He never turned on the light but from his breath, I knew it was my uncle Ron my father's brother. He told me if I yell out, he would kill my whole family then save me for last.

He placed one hand on my tiny chest while he pulled up my nightgown. He didn't even bother to remove my panties; he forced himself inside me. The pain was unbearable I wanted to die right then. I bit down into his hand hard as I could. He was stealing every ounce of innocence my little body had. "God where are you," I was saying to myself. He kept going until he had finished. He removed his hand from my chest and mouth then wiped himself off on my nightgown. He washed the blood from between my legs with a washrag lying on the sink. Once he was sure I had stopped bleeding, he then picked me up and took me back upstairs to Kelly's room. He placed me back into bed, he then reminded me he would kill my family by waving his hand across his throat. The rest of the night, I just laid there shaking all over. Kelly never woke up until our aunt came into the room.

"You girls get up and eat breakfast,"

She said. Taking my time getting out of bed because the pain was so bad to move, I went straight into the bathroom to see if I was still bleeding. There was just a big spot in the center of my panties. When I walked into the kitchen, everyone was already seated at the table. My aunt asked me was I feeling ok, I busted out crying. "What's wrong baby girl," My aunt said.

I looked up at her but, I knew I couldn't tell what happen. What would I do without my mother and father? I would be forced to come live here with this monster. I lied and said I missed my mom. She hugged me while helping me into my chair. Uncle Ron sat across from me just winking his eye. An hour later my father came to pick me up. I ran and grabbed my overnight bag, then got into the car without saying goodbye. I watched my dad and Uncle share a hug. If he only knew what his brother did to me. When he got in the car, he asked why I didn't say goodbye. I just told him I was ready to go home. We didn't talk all the way home. I jumped out the car soon as he pulled into the driveway, I ran fast as I could into the arms of my mother who was standing in the doorway.

"I love you," Was all I kept saying. She picked me up into her arms. The pain was unbearable but I didn't care. I went into my room and changed my blood stain underpants. I stuffed them behind my dresser until I could bury them in the backyard. That night I slept in my parent's bed. Not because I was scared, I kept thinking he would hurt them while I was asleep. Uncle Ron continued molesting me until I was fifteen.

The only reason he stopped, he was killed in a bad car wreck. His death was the first day I felt safe, but the damage to my mind is ongoing. I never saw myself as a decent person again. I felt like it was all my fault. If I just stayed home that weekend. I couldn't even hate Kelly for what happen. I later found out he was doing it to another cousin as well. She was over my house one-day last year. I walked into the bathroom while she was getting dress and noticed a scar on her hip. When I asked about it, she broke down crying. She said Uncle Ron took her the same way he did me. She said he told her he would kill her mom and dad also.

I could see the hurt in her eyes. The scar came from his class ring he used to wear. "It would cut me while he held me down," she said. I asked her when he stopped molesting her; she said when she reached 16. Kelly has lung cancer now. The doctors gave her five years which three have already past. We still trusting God for a full recovery. I never told my family what happen, I made a vow to take it to my grave. Starting to feel in my heart someone could use my testimony. God, if this is your will, please show me the way. A knock on the door again, this is becoming a hot spot. "Hello, we need to use the restroom," A voice called out to me. I forgot where I was for a second. Pushing back the tears, I walked over and unlocked the door.

"So sorry ladies, it was rough coming here today. I needed a minute to get myself together," I said.

"Its fine First Lady Walker, we understand. Just know the whole church is standing with you," One of the ladies replied.

I gather my things and let them have it. Went back inside to the service, they were just about to close things out. I took my seat and just looked up at my dear sweet husband as he was praying. I still couldn't see how God could use the both of us to do his will. The Bible teaches us not to question the Lord but to walk by faith, not by sight. All through the Bible you will find where he uses the most unusable of people to give his people at the appointed time and place what they need. For Pastor Walker and I, this is that place and time. I still struggle with my past because my sexual desires seem always to draw me to a dark place.

Growing up, I never felt like the rest of the other girls when it came to boys. I felt I was only good for sleeping around. Who would want me after everything I had gone through. Going from man to man like it was nothing. Somehow still able to keep it on the low. I learned how to be quiet from Uncle Ron. I became a cheerleader in high school which meant more boys to pass me around. Some of them would call me in/out Kerry because they knew they could get it and go. Wasn't until college I slowed down. That's where I met my wonderful husband. I was just a freshman, and he was my Biology professor. My grades started slipping badly. I needed his class to keep my scholarship so I put my body to use. This time for what I wanted. It felt weird the first few times. My grades went from a D to an A overnight. I started to kick him to the curve, but there was something about him I liked. I would later find out he had a calling to minister instead of teaching. We married my junior year of college. My parents took to him in spite of the age difference. There was an opening back here at the church, we prayed first and the Lord said yes. He has turned things completely around here. Still if the people knew how we hooked up, they would be divided. Still a lot of old school families with closed minds.

If they only knew how he brought me to the Lord. All those Bible study's he made me attend. If he didn't come when he did, I would probably be selling my body for money. How did I allow myself to get caught up with all these men? It's sad that James didn't have any family to say goodbye. Deacon Mosley did an excellent job putting this all together. We still don't know who paid for it all. "Everyone stand please," My husband said. We must be heading to the grave site. The only reason I'm going is to make sure they put his body six feet under the ground. I should not feel this way, but when you have a shotgun put to your head then you can judge me. I turned away as they passed by with the coffin. "Dear, are you ok?" my husband asked as he came and stood beside me.

I told him I was fine. I will be happy when he is six feet under that's all.

"Honey, he's not the same man from that night. He gave his life over to Jesus, and we need to remember only God can judge him now. Take my hand, and let's show the love of the Lord alright."

"Fine, but I'm still not ready to forgive him yet. You are stronger than me in this area," I told him as we walked out.

We made it over to the town cemetery. I tried to stay in the car but my husband did not allow me. The headstone they got was done up nicely I must say. It read, "Redemption is only a breath away." Fitting for the way he gave his life to Christ. Looking over at Frank, I still have strong feelings for him. What if we met in another time and place? I should be ashamed of myself but I'm not. Who knows how long my sweet husband has left to live. I need to keep my options open. Frank moves up beside the coffin. He's about to begin talking. "Does anyone want to say anything before we pray?" He asked.

He waited for a few minutes but no one responded. What could they say? No one really knew him like that. James only brought them pain from the time he hit town. I know what I wanted to say, but they don't have enough words in the dictionary for that. Everyone did show the love of Christ at the end I must say. Guess it's going to be him then. He opens his mouth to talk once more.

"What to say? Do I bring up the drug dealer days of this man? How about his years of being in prison? What about that night he killed a store owner in cold blood? The old James was truly no angel. He could kill you, then have dinner without blinking an eye. I hated the old James, but the Bible says to hate the sin not the sinner. That's one I'm still working at. That night in the hospital, clearly transformation was in his eyes. Old James had passed away; reborn James wanted a chance to live. God saw fit that he was needed and took him. Who am I to second guess the will of the Lord? Just want to thank everyone for coming out today. James didn't have a real family, but in the end, we all accepted him into ours. I will now close in prayer; all heads lowered, please.

Father we are gathered here to say goodbye to a man who is not without his share of sins. We dare not try and judge his faith as to his deeds. We believe the scriptures; he is a newborn Christian now. We come to lay this person to rest Father, and we ask that you welcome him with open arms. I can't account for all the other people he has done evil too but the ones he has crossed paths with now. We all forgive him for all the wrong he has done because you saw fit to spare his soul which I can never thank you enough. I once called this man my enemy; now I'm proud to call him my brother in Christ. I close with these last words. We all should learn from this tragedy. Never to give up on someone based on the lifestyle they live. I'm living proof of your love and mercy. Let all God's people say Amen."

Everyone said, "Amen." Afterwards, we all hugged and began to separate having small conversations amongst ourselves. I wanted to go over and talk to Frank, but I didn't wish to show disrespect. So I stayed close to my husband for now. He never skips an opportunity to preach no matter the occasion. I learn not to cut him off, you never know who maybe in need of a word. He has led people to the Lord at IHOP'S before. I just positioned myself better where I could watch Frank doing his own soul reaching. If I didn't know better, I would think Frank was my husband's son. I wonder if he even notice that I been keeping an eye on him this whole time. My husband is walking over to him now; I'll just stay right over here until he comes back.

## FRANK

Kerry sure looks great in her black dress. Almost forgot how much I feel for her. She's like a black widow spider. You see her coming but her beauty mesmerizes you. Her sting is like no other; her venom is lethal to anyone caught in her web. Kind of feel sorry for Pastor Walker, but he said he knows his wife. When I walked into the room to save Kerry, I didn't know what the outcome was going to be. I just didn't want to lose her. I was willing to give my life for a woman who could care less about mine. Guess when you're caught up, you will do just about anything.

I found my place here, and hopefully a better life than the one I left. I had said a few words before they lowered James to his final resting place. People may be wondering how I paid for everything, It was with the money James had stashed inside my sofa. If my cell phone had not slipped down into it, I would never have known it was there. It's only fitting that the money is used for this.

"Deacon Mosley that was an excellent service you gave this young man."

"Thank you, Pastor. I just let the Holy Spirit lead me. Just wish he could have had family present."

"Once he give his life to Christ, we all became his family. I know what you mean, now what are your plans for the future Deacon?"

"I'm hoping to continue being a member of this community."

"Just what I wanted to hear son. I know it's going to take time getting past everything that occurred, please don't spend too much time doing the, would of, could of, should of thing. We need you working at the church ok."

I laughed a little for the first time in days. You're right as always Pastor; I'll get right on my Sunday school lessons." He gives me a firm hug while praying for me. Still can't take my eyes off of Kerry, we still have unfinished business to settle. James death didn't change anything about that; I motioned with my free hand to let her know just that.

"Well Deacon, Let me get my wife to the house. I know she didn't want to be here." He said as he was walking away. I hung around until they filled the grave. Everyone that came had already headed to their vehicles.

While waiting, a text message from Kerry comes over my cell phone. She wants to meet later tonight; I knew she couldn't change overnight. This time, I will stand my ground. We need to end this for good. There are plenty of single women in town to choose, but I'm too young to be talking about settling down right now. It just dawned on me that I didn't see Officer Jones at the service, guess he had enough of James in his town. I sure didn't see her and him together. When I say she's good, that's an understatement. I tossed in a small pocket Bible into James coffin at the church. Don't have this afterlife thing down yet. I do believe what it says about being absent from the body, is to be present with the Lord.

You never know if your enemies will see Christ before you. If James could get in, there is still hope for all of us still above ground. They just tossed in the last shovel full of dirt, now I can get back to living without watching my back. It took me days to clean up my apartment. Officer Jones was able to set up a meeting with the DA. He contacted the DA office back in Detroit; they agreed to drop the charges after hearing what happen.

Pastor Walker also spoke with the DA; he told them all about the new man I had become. Before hanging up, they wished me well. The DA also said he was sorry for not letting me come home to bury my mother. I guess dropping the charges was his way of making atonement for them dropping her in a hole and just pushing dirt over her body. I don't even know if they had a casket. Doesn't even matter now. She's in a better place than where she was.

## Pastor Walker

"Honey, you feeling ok," I asked Kerry as she was sitting there with a lost look on her face. Just drive the car please she told me. This James ordeal has done a number on her while almost giving me a heart attack. Knowing she was almost killed, reminded me of the love I have for her. When she came running into my arms, nothing else mattered.

I would have given up everything just to spend one more day with her. Don't get me wrong, the church is my world. I love being a pastor, but without Kerry to share it with me, I couldn't preach as I do now. Somehow the pain she causes me is the spark that fuels my messages. As a preacher, we never know where the inspiration for that next message will come. Unfortunately for me that has not been the case. I tried to hold her hand that was resting on the center console, but she just pulled it back down to her lap. We were almost to the house. "I'll run you a bath, and get you a nice glass of wine," I told her. She started rubbing my leg. "Tell you what I want sweetheart," She replied.

"Anything you need my dear just ask."

"I would love to go over and visit my cousin tonight if that's ok?"

I turned to look out my window before responding to her request. "I did want to spend quality time with my wife, but that would be good for you both. How is she doing with the chemo treatments?"

"She has her good days and bad days. Thanks for understanding."

I hate her using her cousin like that. She knew that was a situation where I could not say no. When you been running game long as she has, you know what buttons to push. We made it to the house without further conversation. She went straight into the kitchen to fix dinner before changing. She came back downstairs wearing jeans and a sweater. She kept it conservative so I wouldn't get second thoughts.

"Honey your plate is on the stove, I'll be back soon as I can."

"Be careful on the road, you know how you love to speed," I said.

She left out the house giving me a light kiss on the cheek. I walked over to the window and watched to see which car she was taking. I didn't care, but if she was cheating, I didn't want the smell of another man in my vehicle. Good, she is taking hers. I walked down the hall to my study. I picked up my Bible and begin to converse with the Lord. "Lord, this is your servant Bishop Henry Walker. I come to you because I don't know what else to do. I love my wife Kerry, and I cannot see my life without her in it. I know she is not going to see her cousin. Whoever the man is this time, I pray you will touch his heart Lord. I wish no ill will on no one Father, I'm just sick and tired of being sick and tired. Kerry has been this way from the day we met. Who am I to be telling you? Guess I'm trying to convince myself. In spite of our age difference, I was sure we could make it work.

Silly old man, what were you thinking? You rolled the dice and came up short. Lord, I don't know how much life I have left in this old broken down body. I just ask that my work in your name is not in vain. If loving my wife is keeping me from everlasting life, Father, please forgive us both. Knowing that putting a ring on her finger doesn't change the sin and it sure didn't change Kerry. Walking around this big house is starting to feel more cold and empty.

Maybe if we had children, things would have been different. I wish I knew more about her childhood. Every time I bring up the subject, she goes on the attack. Whatever happen must have damaged her badly. I even notice it when we are intimate. She is so beautiful on the outside, how could the inside be so messed up? She still takes my breath away everytime I look at her. On the inside, she must be fighting a million demons. Wasn't until I went and got a copy of our cell phone bill, I learned she was cheating on me. It was shocking to find out how many men were involved.

She stopped after I confronted her two years ago. She had a private number I was unaware of. I was even thinking about placing a tracking device on her car, but that would just put a wall between us. I'll just keep the faith as any man would do. Just to add to my faith, let me go up here and look through her things. I walked up the spiral staircase to the second floor. She doesn't like it when I rummage around her stuff. Sure doesn't help my psyche to say the lease. At my age, the talk of a divorce will never be an option. To death do us part is the only way I am leaving this marriage. Would I put up a fight over Kerry? Hopefully it won't come to that. I took a few pics with my phone, that way I could put everything back like it was. After not finding anything, I put everything back while looking at the pics I took. I went back down to my study. Changing the topic now, thank you Lord for Deacon Mosley. That young man was truly sent right on time. With me getting to that point where a successor will have to be named, he makes the right choice right now. His hunger for you is like none I have seen before. That testimony he gave was so convincing. The way he shows me nothing but respect which is rear in young people these days.

I'll keep imparting all you have given me into his mind. I feel I can completely trust him around Kerry. Every time they are near each other, I don't sense nothing but friendship. If I'm wrong, then I must be slipping in my old age. Still makes me angry when I think of her and Deacon Smith. Caught them together in the church storage building two years ago, he tried to tell me they were looking for some old files. Kerry just pushed past me and walked off. I dismissed him from the church right then. Don't want to start even getting those images in my head. Deacon Mosely is going to make a great preacher someday. Just hope he can stay the course. He is still a newborn baby in all this which is perfect because his mind has not had time to take on a bunch of foolishness. I'm going to bed now, thanks for hearing the rambling of an old man." When I was done, I took a long shower before getting into bed.

## KERRY

I just laughed as I was walking out the door. I must have at least ten tickets this month alone. When you got a judge on your list of admirers, tickets don't mean a thing. I give him a light kiss on the cheek, didn't want to mess up my lips. I took my BMW because I always keep an overnight bag in the truck. Never know when I'll have to change clothes.

I texted Frank the location I wanted him to meet me. He might feel this is too soon after everything that has happened, but I could care less about that. I want what I want plus; I don't take no for an answer. I made it to the park where Frank and I had our last conversation. Don't see him anywhere, he better not stand me up after I lied to get out. I see car lights coming from down the road, let me get back to the car in case it's not him. I have a gun, but I'm scared to carry it around. With my anger toward men, I would shoot someone. Yes, that's his car. He is so proud of that Deacon Mosley plate on the front. I get back out and stand in front of my car. "I was just about to leave. What took you so long?"

"Don't start ok Kerry. I had to pray before agreeing to this meeting."

"Why? I just want to talk."

"With all we been through, the last thing we should be is alone together. Look at the way you're dress for one thing."

"It's just jeans and a top, what's sexy about this?" I said while moving closer to him.

"Please, with your figure in those tight jeans. That top is almost see through. Pastor Walker let you come out the house looking this way?" He said taking two steps backward.

"He thinks I'm with my sister. I changed tops in the car."

"Great more lies. Now, what did you want to meet about?"

"Don't put this all on me. You gave me that hand jester at the grave site while my sweet husband was giving you a hug at that."

She's right. Look at her in them jeans, I want to rip them off. She knows that top is driving me crazy. The nerve of her wearing that perfume I like. Devil get from behind me, I feel you trying to push me closer to her.

"Look Kerry, I do want you in my life."

"But what Frank? I see it in your eyes. Tell me you want to give all we had up."

"I'm holding fast that God has something bigger than this for me. I sold drugs, been shot and stabbed. I have been to prison, lived in the worst conditions unimaginable; still he showed favor to me. Jesus, his Son, died for people like me. Wow!! I just want to tell the world. I want to be that living testimony for other's living that thug life. They don't have to stay confined to the world of pain and heartbreak," He said.

I started to clap loudly. "That was rich, where do I drop my offering? I didn't come way out here to go to church. Anything else preacher man? What now, you are going to save little on

Kerry all by your lonesome. Don't waste your time, I know the real you."

"Kerry, Say what you feel now. After today, we won't be having this conversation again. I'm a new person whether you believe in me or not. You are my sister in Christ, the wife of my Pastor and the First Lady of the church. I see only this person now. Whatever evil you carried from your past to now, I will help you deal with it. I extend the hand of friendship, take it or leave it. The choice is your's." I stood there looking him over, the person who is standing before me is not my old Frank. God has truly taken over his life. His eyes burn right through mine like he's looking into my soul. I find myself trying to cover up. I know now, we will never cross this path again. Goodbye, old Frank. Hello, Deacon Frank Mosley. I'm about to do something I never did in my life. Not even with my own husband. Trust a man. "I'm so sorry, my lust for you over- shadowed my clear thinking of what is Godly. I see the Lord in you, and I have seen it for some time now. Being selfish has almost cost me a real friend. Can we start over please? Hello, my name is First Lady Walker. It's good to meet you Deacon Mosley."

"The pleasure is all mine First lady. Thank you Kerry. I don't want to lose the connection we gained."

"I'm letting my guard down with you, don't let me regret this."

"I won't. Maybe one day when the time is right, you will tell me your story. I can see the hurt all over you. Lord knows I saw your wrath when you get mad."

We both laughed. He has no idea what he just asked me. Should I allow him to come in that deep? Would he understand my pain? I don't see him as a person who would try to exploit it. My parents don't even know. I need to talk to my cousin first. If she dies, I would be the only one left to bear this pain. We have tried to forgive Uncle Ron, but the traumatic experience has scarred us for life. "Frank, let's take things slow. We just agreed to be just friends. We both know that it won't be easy. You already crossed over to a place not even my husband knows. Trust. Don't dig any deeper right now, I don't want to start building a wall between us."

"I understand. I didn't mean to pry, guess I'll be going now. See you at church Mrs. Walker." I watched him drive away; it was like part of me is being dragged behind that car. I visualized us driving off into the sunset, putting all this behind us living our dreams. Didn't take long for me to come back to the real world when I heard something moving in the bushes. I jumped in the car so fast; you would have taught I was running track. If I go back home this early, he's going to suspect something. Let me give my Kelly a call. "Hey Lady, How you feeling?" I said when she picked up. "Kerry, what in the world are you doing?"

"What you talking about, can't I call my cousin?"

"Kerry, if you're using me to get out the house, don't you think I should know? Henry called me half hour ago; he wanted to make sure

34

you arrived ok. He said he tried your cell phone, but it went straight to voicemail. I could hear in his voice that he was worried."

"What did you tell him Kelly?"

"I told him you went to Walgreens to pick up my prescriptions, and I would make sure you called him when you arrived."

"Girl, thank you so much. I forgot to call you when I left the house."

"Don't be thanking me. You know how I feel about your creeping. Henry has been nothing but good to you. He is a Man of God, and I'm not trying to bust hell gates wide open with you. When are you going to stop using what Uncle Ron did to us affect your life? Please come over and see me," She pleaded. "Girl bye!!" I said as I hung up. She is right, I'm using my past to dictate my future. Let me turn this car around, hearing her cry didn't help the situation. If anything was to happen to her because of me, I could never forgive myself. Kelly's fight with lung cancer keeps her mind away from her past. The

Lord does work in mysterious ways. Why did he allow her to get cancer and me to get caught up with so many men? Sure the Bible teaches us, He will never put more on us then we can bear. I could never bear what she is going through. I probably would have committed suicide by now.

Kelly kept it to herself for years. She had married before I did which I didn't learn until I came back here to live. His name is Rodney. He's 6'1, with light brown hair, blue eyes, medium build. He has that distinctive look like a male model, but he's in real estate which helps pays for her health care. They have this grand old Victorian style home. Kelly is real old fashioned and lives a conservative lifestyle. We both have strong Christian beliefs, I just let mine teeter on the fence every day. Yes, I know the Lord doesn't want us to be lukewarm. What is that Bible verse my husband preaches? Now I remember it's in the book of Revelation chapter 3 verse 16. *"So then because you are lukewarm, and neither cold nor hot, I will spew you out of my mouth."*

You would think, well as I know that scripture, I would change my ways. She won't tell me how they met, I just know he's the best thing to happen to her. We kind of lost touch for a while when I went off to college. Me being a freshman on a campus full of men didn't help the situation any. Before I knew it, I was going to all the frat parties given. I was living the wild life for sure. She never approved of my life choices. Every time I would call her, I got the same old speech about change my ways before something bad happens.

She started sounding like a mother instead of my sweet cousin. I cut back on calling and totally stop taking her calls. Eventually, we drifted apart. It wasn't until I moved back home that we started hanging out again. Things are much better between us, and the bond we share has never been stronger. She is still not happy about my life choices, we just agree to disagree about them. Another ten minutes I should be there. Let me fix my face because thinking about her got me all teared up.

# KELLY

I feel so bad for what happen to my cousin Kerry and I pray for her each day. My life maybe coming to an end soon. I can't dwell on my past because I don't have the time nor the energy. I will recall that day Uncle Ron took my innocence for the last time hopefully. I was only nine years old, I enjoyed everything about life. You never caught me without a big smile on my face. Both my parents lived together, and they loved each other so much.

My father treated her like she was the only woman in the world. That was until I came along. I had my dad wrapped around my little finger. Watching them, I knew one day this would be me. We never went to bed without praying together. "A family that prays together stays together," My father always said. I was the only child; that was good but sometimes lonely. Kerry was more of a sister than a cousin in my life. I was what they called a latchkey kid. Meaning I was given a key to the house. I was to come straight home and not let anyone inside. It was a hot day on a Friday. We only had three more days of school left for the year. I couldn't wait for summer break; that meant Kerry would be able to stay over longer. I came home as usual; I made sure to lock the door behind me. My folks called to make sure I was ok, they both said they loved me. I felt safe being in the house alone.

About an hour later, there was a knock at the door. I went upstairs to look out the window; it was my Uncle Ron. He is one of my father's brother. I didn't think anything of it and ran down to the front door. I loved my uncle because he was always bringing me gifts. He loved to bounce me on his lap which my mother started saying something about it. She said I was getting too old for that. I was an early bloomer; she would explain to me. He said he wanted to use the restroom; I told him I wasn't allowed to let anyone in the house. He said we were family so I did. I was standing with my back turned in the hallway, he put his hand over my mouth and took me to the basement. He closed the door behind him. I tried screaming, but it didn't work. He pulled my dress up and raped me.

Afterward, he told me, "I'll kill your parents and make you watch if you tell anyone." He then made me give him the things I had on. Placing them in a trash bag, he watched me take a shower then he cleaned up the bathroom. He waited until I stopped crying before he left. I was hurting so bad that I curled up on the bed. My mother came home first later that day. I wiped the tears away before she came into the kitchen where I was sitting. "What's wrong baby girl," she asked. That's because I was sitting at the kitchen table doing my homework. She would almost have to beat me to do it. I just looked up and smiled. I knew if I opened my mouth, I would break down crying.

My father came home later that night. I was already in the bed. He brought my mother to my room, we prayed and he gave me a kiss on the forehead. I cried the rest of the night. The next day I went to school as if nothing had happened. When it was time for me to go home, I would start shaking all over. The closer I got to my house, I wet myself. I checked all the doors three times before I felt safe. It was months later before my mother noticed I stop wearing dresses. To this day, I won't wear a dress unless I have to. My uncle is dead but the fear is still there. I thank God for my wonderful husband. He came into my life just when I was about to give up. I parked on the bridge overlooking the river; I got out my car right after writing a goodbye note. I just couldn't deal with the pain anymore.

Right before I was about to jump in when I heard a voice call out to me. "You are not alone." He ran over and pulled me back. He didn't ask what was wrong; he just wanted to know what I needed to keep living. He has never left my side from that day forward. I encourage anyone dealing with hidden issues to get the help you deserve. Don't let someone else control your destiny. This cancer is taking my life, but it will never steal my joy. I never had kids, but a daughter would have been nice. See how you can allow fear to rob you of the blessings of life.

Let me pull myself together before Kerry gets here. She doesn't know the complete story of my pain.

"Hey there Rodney, where is my cousin?"

"She should be upstairs resting I hope. Please don't stay too long ok."

"That's what I love about you, always looking after her. Thank you."

"Get on up there before you go to crying."

"Knock, knock," She said while opening the door. "Come on in here silly. Didn't think you were coming."

"Kelly, I keep forgetting Rodney is white. He acts more like a brother."

"I say the same thing to myself all the time. So tell me all about it."

"All about what?" She replied.

"Don't play dumb, I know you were with Frank. You would think that night at the church made an impact."

"Kelly it did. I saw my whole life flash before my eyes."

"Then why were you out with Frank? You should be home with that man who loves you."

"Don't judge me. You of all people know my story. I can't keep myself away from him."

"That's another thing, please stop using what happen to account for your sins. I'm so tired of hearing that song."

"Wow Kelly, I'll charge that to your head and not to your heart. What you better than me now? Because you don't do dirt behind Rodney's back, I guess cancer prevented that from happing!!" I put my hands over my eyes and started to cry. "Oh my Lord! Kelly, you know I didn't mean that. Please stop crying," She said as Rodney was knocking at the door.

"Honey, you all right in there!" He yelled out.

"Yes dear, we just had a little disagreement that's all," I replied.

"Kerry, please don't get her upset," He said in a stern voice.

"I won't and sorry for getting loud in your home." We waited until we heard him going back down the stairs. "Look Kerry, maybe we should change the subject."

"It's fine. I did meet with Frank."

"How did it go? Did you both do the nasty?" I said in the hope of brightening the mood.

"Look at my big cousin, you do have a dark side." We both couldn't help but laugh. Even though I hated what she was doing, I lived vicariously through her encounters. "Girl, he dumped me."

"You ok with that Kerry?"

"Sure. I'll just pull up my big girl panties and move on."

"No you won't, I can see it all over you. Don't allow this man to ruin your marriage, and don't you mess up his new life here."

"We agreed to remain friends. I'm sure I can handle that part. We just have to wait and see where this all leads. Enough about me and my men troubles. How are you feeling?"

"I have been feeling more like myself these days. I have been reading these Christian fiction Books. They allow me to escape from my sickness. The messages of hope in them is just what I need right now. You should read one for yourself."

"Maybe I'll do just that. Well, I was told not to stay long."

"Let me guess, my hubby right."

"Yes. He's right because we need you around. Now give me a kiss so I can leave." We shared a long hug, and I told Rodney goodnight as I was leaving out. Good thing I already changed back into my other top, not safe for a woman to be pulling over this late. Maybe I should have called Henry. He's not going to raise a fuss. That side-eye thing he does is bad enough. Good thing it's only 11:30 pm. I'll just call Kelly while I'm walking in the door and put her on speaker too. That one always works for me. I don't see the bedroom light on, old behind must have dose off already. I have to increase his vitamins. I dialed Kelly while going to the door.

"All right girl, I'm in the house safe and sound. It was good spending time with you too. Love you. Bye." If he's still up, I know he had to hear that. Shoot, I'm starving, let's see what leftovers we got. Little of this, a whole lot of that, top it off with a nice glass of wine. I'll just go into the living room. Why is it so dark in here? Old fart turned off all the lights. "I got your old fart sweetheart." light on the coffee table comes on.

"How long you been sitting in the dark?"

"Does it matter, but if you must know about three hours. I have been in prayer for you. Kerry, I'm not going to ask where you been. The truth is not your best attribute so spare me the lie. Just glad you made it home safely dear. Enjoy your snack, I'm going to bed now."

What just happen? All the nights I been coming in late, this is the first time he stayed up waiting for me. Praying for me until I came home, what's that about? How naïve of me, almost forgot that look in his eyes that night. I never saw him so scared in my life. How that black man loves me so much. I stayed in the living room for a while. I had to let tonight's event settle in my head. The world as I knew it was getting smaller. He knows something but what? Foolish woman, how long did you think you could keep this up.

I would usually talk to Frank about what is going on. He understands me more than anyone I been with over the years. I love my husband don't get me wrong, but something keeps telling me that Frank is my soul mate. I went up to take a shower. He may read into that but I need a shower. I gathered my things and went into the bathroom. I turned the shower on not because I'm ready to take a shower, but I needed to drown out the tears. As I stepped into the shower, my eyes began their waterworks. For me, this is getting to be an ongoing scenario. The tears I mean. The old Kerry would never shed a tear over any man. Instead, I would have them so broken, they would pull out their own heart if I told them. After tonight, this is going to be my last cry for a while. In the morning, I'm back to being the boss chick in this town. When I came out, he was sound asleep. I just said my prayers and went to sleep.

*******

# Frank

I'm so glad it's Sunday morning because after dealing with Kerry, I need some word. After turning on my Keurig, I threw a microwavable breakfast sandwich in the microwave. I need to learn to cook, all this process food can't be good for me. After my quick meal, I finished getting ready then headed over to the church. I need to get there early due to I'm preaching this morning. My sermon today will be based on reconciliation.

The Lord put that in my spirit last week. I'm hoping it will convict Kerry into turning over a new leaf. As I pulled into the parking lot, I'm glad to see not to many cars. I started laughing when I saw Mother Mary's car. I don't think I ever beat her to a Sunday service. I parked in the same parking space the day James found me. I guess that was my way of getting back on that horse. I went straight into the pastor's office to make sure the thermostat is on 62 degrees. It's hot out today, plus he doesn't like to get to hot. I would think with his old bones he would prefer the heat. Let me straighten up his desk and check his refrigerator.

Pastor Walker doesn't want an armor-bearer; he said a healthy man should be able to carry their own Bible. So we just make sure to check things as much as possible. When I finished, I went into one of the classrooms to go back over my sermon. I was only studying for a few minutes when I heard someone coming down the hallway. Maybe one of the teachers coming to set up for their class.

"Well, good morning Deacon Mosely. It's good to see you son. What brings you here this early?"

"Good morning Mother Mary, it's good to see you too. I'm preaching this morning."

"Sounds good and what is your text," She asked. "I will be talking on Reconciliation. The Lord placed it in my spirit last week."

"That sounds like it's going to be a good message. Well, I won't keep you any longer."

She gives me a motherly hug and heads out. Just when I was about to go back to my sermon, she was walking back into the room. "Yes mother, did you forget something?"

"You mind if I talk to you for a second?" She said. Of course I knew it won't be a second.

"Why no mother. Please have a seat." I get up and pull out her chair then retake mine. "So what's on your mind mother?"

"Now you know I'm not a big talker, just need you to hear me out."

"Yes ma'am. I'm all ears because your words are wisdom to my soul."

"I haven't had a chance to talk to you since that ordeal. When I was asked not to come to the church that night, I didn't even have to think about it. There was no devil in hell going to keep me from the house of God. I'm a season Christian, time and season tested. I have been through more storms than I care to recall along with the other mothers. I prayed my husband, children, grandchildren and a host of others through. If the devil wants a battle, he picked the right church to attack. Let me get back to what I wanted to say before I break out in praise and worship right now."

She was almost coming out of her chair. I was moving out the way because I saw it coming. When Mother Marry gets her praise going, you better look out.

"Well, I did lose my train of thought. Son, I just want you to know that I will always be in your corner. Don't let this life the Lord has given you go to waste. Yes, there will be times in your walk that storms are coming because you can't be a Christian without them. There is no get out of storm cards in the Bible. Son, you just stay anchored in that bible and get your prayer life up. Those two things will help you when they do come. I leave you with this verse. Psalms 55:22, *"Cast thy burden upon the Lord, and he shall sustain thee: he shall never suffer the righteous to be moved."*

As always mother walks away leaving you to meditate on her words of wisdom. I was able to get in a good half hour of studying before the Sunday school teacher walked in. I knew the kids wouldn't be too long behind her so I headed upstairs to the sanctuary for Deacon Jones's Bible School lesson. After about an hour, the praise team went up to get service started. I returned to the pastor's office because I knew he would be there. I knocked on the door before going straight in.

"Well Good Morning Deacon Mosely. Are you just getting here?"

"Good Morning Pastor. I been here for a while now. I just came down from Sunday school."

"Great, I know it was good. Have a seat I wanted to talk to you before you preached today."

"Is everything alright Pastor? You still want me to preach today?"

"Of course, why wouldn't I? Just want to be sure that you won't be distracted being this will be your first time preaching since that day.

When you look out over the congregation, you may only see James out there."

"Pastor that never crossed my mind. Yes, that was a bad night but it's the outcome that matters more. James brought hell to the house of God, but His goodness and mercy filled every inch of this place. When the dust settled, it even filled the heart of James. So when I look over the congregation, I will only see what the power of the word of God can do."

"Deacon Mosely, for a young man that's only been a Christain a short time, you have so much wisdom. I had expected you to say there was still concern about today. The words you shared only confirmed my decision in making you a deacon of this church. There is much for you to learn as a deacon, but I want you to start taking on the mindset of an Elder. I know it's still early for that being your still getting settled in you roll. Well, it's time to go up and feed the people of God."

We walked up together then took our seats. The praise team had everyone in high praise and worship. It wasn't long before I was caught up in the spirit myself. Pastor Walker went up to the podium. "Good morning, welcome everyone to the Road to Redemption Church of God where we focus on the power of forgiveness. We like to welcome all our first-time visitors. There are no new announcements this morning, just remember to keep each other in prayer. I know most of you came anticipating me to preach this morning," He said.

People started talking amongst themselves trying to guess who was preaching. They knew we didn't have a guest this week. Pastor raised his hands to get everyone to settle back down.

"People of God, please settle down. I may not be preaching on today. Nevertheless, our very own Deacon Mosely, who we all love will be bringing the word this morning. So stand on your feet and welcome him as he comes!!"

Starting with Mother Mary, everyone jumped to their feet clapping and shouting. I went up and placed my things down on the podium. Pastor Walker laid his hand on my shoulder as he passed to reassure me. When I raised my head, the first face I came into contact with was Mother Mary. This time, she looked diffident. Her face looked like my mother's face. She was making eye contact with me like when I used to get scared when I heard my father coming through the front door. She then told me its ok son, I'm right here with you. I shook my head then looked again. This time, I saw Mother Mary's face. Right then, I knew my mother was still with me in spirit.

"People of God, let us pray. Father, I ask this morning that I decrease that you may increase. Let the Holy Spirit go forth and comfort your people. Empower my message to give hope and encouragement to the broken hearted. I ask that you reassure those that are walking around in total darkness. Let them know that they are not alone. In Jesus name, Amen."

Everyone shouted Amen in agreement. "My text this Morning is on Reconciliation. Imagine that two friends who were close from birth and as they grew, they became inseparable. They shared great conversation and could confide in each other no matter what the hour. Then one day something happens that causes faith in the other to fade. They slowly drift apart until they become almost a whisper in each other's life. One of them tries everything in their power to reconcile with the other, but walls went up around the others heart that it becomes unreachable. Now they missed out on all the wonderful experiences they could have shared together. Family, trips, new births born into the world, marriages, graduations, promotions and the list goes on.

Now the only time one recognizes the other, is at the worst times in their life. It's only to find fault in why things aren't going so good. They turn to the world looking for new friends only to find a few true ones. They quickly learn the grass isn't as green on the other side as they thought. Then when they are at the lowest of lows in their life, who reaches out to show love. Not the world they ran to for support, but that one friend who never left. See they never had a problem with you, and they knew that the storm you both were going through would pass. They don't ask any questions when you call, they just say come home friend I never left you. See people of God, that's just what the Lord is saying today. I never left you so come on home. All you have to do is call out and I will reconcile with you. Then we can pick up where we left off. Open your Bibles to 2 Corinthians chapter 5 verse 19. It reads, **"To wit, that God was in Christ, reconciling the world unto himself, not imputing trespasses unto them; and hath committed unto us the word reconciliation."**

I now close with asking anyone that would like to come down and reconcile with the Lord saved or unsaved. The invitation is open, will there be one." As I was closing, people began making their way down to the front as the praise team song. I looked back at Pastor Walker for direction. He walked up and told me he would come down with me, but he wanted me to pray for each person individually.

So we headed down the steps toward them. I prayed for each one just as he asked me to. He helped me when it came time to lead people to Christ. I didn't want to make a mistake with someone's salvation. When service was over, ten people gave their lives to Christ. First Lady Walker led them out to give them some information. I stayed behind with Pastor greeting the congregation.

Afterwards, he gave his blessing of approval of the message I gave. I went back up to gather my things then headed for the parking lot. Mother Marry was sitting in her car just behind mine.

"Deacon Mosley, you know I was not leaving without telling you my thoughts," She said with a big smile. I just smiled and waited for her response. "Deacon that was a strong word son. I just want you to keep building your prayer life as we talked about earlier. I see you bringing many souls to the Lord, and that means the devil is going to try and attack your mind. I'll be doing my usual praying on your behalf. Now I got to be going. I got to get my Sunday dinner started; be blessed now."

She pulled off while giving me a wave. I got in my car feeling good about what I did to encourage people instead of hurting them when I sold drugs. Thank you Lord for never forsaking me, and showing me the goodness of your grace. I made it home to get me a much-needed nap. I had only been down for about a half hour when I heard a knock at the door. Who could this be on a Sunday? I got up and went to the door.

"Yes, can I help you please?" No one replied so I asked again. "Yes, who is out there!" Still no one answered. I reached over and got a baseball bat I kept by the door. I never moved so it maybe one of James's folks seeking retaliation for his death. These doors' don't come with a peephole which don't make sense because of the neighborhood this is. Cops come through on the regular. I planted one foot back so I could get a swing then I opened the door. I immediately dropped the bat I was holding, it went rolling toward the wall. My mouth fell open as I stood frozen in time. "Hello. Are you going to say something or just stand there looking ridiculous?" She said.

I couldn't believe my eyes as to who was standing at my front door. I managed to pull myself to together to speak. "Stacy, what in the world are you doing here and how did you locate me?"

"Can we at least come in before all the questions or did we come at a bad time?"

"Of course please come inside. Don't mind the mess, I haven't had a chance to clean up yet," I replied.

As they walked passed me, I was happy to see Stacy but my eyes stayed focused on the 3 feet 2-inch little person who accompanied her.

"Well don't I get a hug Frank? It has been a while?" She said.

"Stacy, please forgive my demeanor. I'm just trying process this right now. My brain hasn't caught up with my eyes just yet."

I walked over and embraced her while keeping my eyes on the child standing beside her. "That's better. Now did that kill you? I see you can't keep your eyes off this lovely lady right here. So let's sit down because I know you have a lot of questions."

"Yes, please have a seat where are my manners. Can I get either of you something to drink?"

"Frank please sit down and stop acting like a nervous wreck. You are scaring the child."

"Yes, your right. Please tell me who this sweet little lady is." I braced myself for the answer.

"Frank Mosely, say hello to Gabrielle Melody Mosley," She said.

When she said that, it was like time stood still. I was speechless. "Frank would you please say something for heaven sake."

"Stacy, I don't know what to say. Are you saying to me what I think you mean?" I stood up and starting pacing around the room. "Yes Frank, this is your daughter. Now please let me explain."

"Yes Stacey, please explain how almost two years later, you show up at my front door with a little girl. Then you look me in my face and tell me I'm the father. How is that?"

"Frank, I tried to tell you when you came home from prison. You didn't even want to be bothered with me. After I had stood by you faithfully, you cut me out of your life just like that. Well, maybe now you will listen because I'm not going anywhere. I found out I was pregnant right before you went to prison. I missed my period, so I went and picked up a pregnancy test from CVS. It was positive which explained the morning sickness. I was on my way to tell you when I saw them putting you in the police car. I was hoping the news would get you to change, and we could get married and be a happy family," She explained.

Now that I think of it, she was throwing up a lot. I thought it was just bad Chinese food like last time. "So why didn't you tell me when you found out? You do know how to write don't you?"

"Frank, I was scared that you would say it wasn't yours or I was trying to hem you up with a baby," She replied.

Is she kidding me right now? Stacy and I were always together unless I was hustling. "I'm sorry you felt that way. Did I come off that cold-blooded?"

"Yes Frank you did. Even I was scared of you, and you know I don't back down from no one. I didn't tell you because I didn't want that weight on you. I knew it was more important for you to keep your head." I walked over and sat down beside her. "You did always watch my back. I would never disrespect you or deny our child. She is beautiful like her mother. Don't think I missed that her middle name is my mother's. Can I hold her?"

"I felt it was fitting, and you could have some part of your mother with you always. Of course you can hold her. Come here Gabrielle and say hello to your father."

She was sitting on the floor watching TV. Watching her walk over to where we were sitting brought tears to my eyes. In her cute white dress with her matching shoes. Her hair was in curls. She is my flesh and blood. Better yet, this is my daughter. The moment she walked into my arms, and I picked her up looking into her eyes I felt complete. I couldn't hold back the tears from dripping on her dress.

"Are you ok daddy? Why are you crying?" She said while wiping her little fingers across my face.

"Stacy she can talk. She just called me daddy!"

"Of course she can silly. She'll be two in three weeks," She said tearing up herself.

Stacy got up and ran into the bathroom crying.


**\*\*\*\*\*\*\*\*\*\***

## Stacy

I ran into the bathroom because I didn't want my daughter to see me cry. I know she's only two, but even her emotions must be running high. Looking at myself in this mirror, I see a 5'6, slim, 24-year-old brown skin complexion female with brown eyes. My hair was braided going down my back, but I had it cut short before I came down. I have been in my share of street fights. Luckily none show on my smooth clear face.

Did I make the right decision on coming here? In some ways, I didn't have a choice. I'm so scared to tell Frank his Connect was the reason I left Detroit. They came looking for him at my place. With this new life, he must have forgotten what the street code is. You either get down or lay down. How they connected us and found me, I have no idea. Who am I fooling, everybody knows there are no real friends in this life. When they kicked in my door, I was coming up the stairs with Gabrielle. When I heard them, I sat her down on the steps and ran up to make sure. When I knew for sure it was my door, I ran back down grabbing her while still running. Good thing I took the money out the apartment two days prior. I don't see any signs of a female staying here which is good for her sake. Well Stacy, get it together you can't stay in here forever. I went back into the living room to find them playing on the floor. Watching them, you would think they never lost a day. "Hello you two, did you miss me?"

"Mommy, look what daddy gave me." He had given her a little toy car.

"Oh, that is so sweet. Now you sit right here and play sweetie. Mommy and daddy need to talk." We walked back over to the sofa. "Are you ok Stacy? You looked troubled about something."

"Frank, I need to tell you a few things as to why I'm here."

"Whatever the reason is, I'm just glad the Lord brought us back to together."

"Let's just hope you feel that way when this conversation is over. Let me finish before you say anything."

"Stacy, stop with the stalling and tell it already."

"Well, first I had to leave with just the clothes on our back. We came home finding you're connect kicking in my door. I was so scared, I just took Gabrielle and ran. I wasn't going to come here but I didn't know where else to go. I heard about what happen to James at the hair salon. That's how I knew where to find you. I just knew if anyone could keep us safe it would be you. Plus how could I keep you from your child. I didn't even get to say goodbye to my mother. I didn't want to lead them to her because I would blame myself if they hurt her or my little brother. If you are wondering about the money, I have all of it outside in the truck of the car. I only spent my own money. I came here hoping you would change your mind and come back. Now you know everything."

"Stacy, I adjusted to my new life so fast, I plum forgot about my old lifestyle. The drug connect, and I forgot about the money I owed. You sure they didn't hurt you or my child. If they touched one hair on either of your heads!"

"Calm down, I told you we got out before they found us."

"Your right. I just need to think about how to resolve this so I won't have to go back to prison. First thing, you both are not going anywhere. Now that I have you back in my life, I'm not going to lose you again. Next, let's get that money out the car. This is not the best of neighborhoods. Give me a second to change then we'll drive over and check you out of that hotel."

"Frank, are you sure you want us to stay with you? I didn't come here to be a charity case or burden on you." I just gave her a tight embraced to reassure her then headed to the bedroom.

# Frank

I went into the bedroom closing the door. Not because I was worried about Stacy seeing me, I just wanted a moment to seek God's wisdom and direction in this matter. I can't allow the Devil to use this situation to pull me backwards. I need to let Stacy see God through the life that I lead. When I was done seeking God, I went over to the mirror. "Frank you're a father. Wow," I said out loud. After I had changed into something more relaxing, I went back into the living room with Stacy and Gabrielle.

"Sorry it took so long. You both ready to go?"

"Yes. Why are you walking like that?" We busted out laughing before heading out the door. I didn't notice I had my chest pumped up.

"What hotel are you staying at Stacy?" I asked. "Do you know where the Hi Mont Hotel is? We are in room 316. While I was sleeping, I kept getting this feeling like you were in the room."

"I stayed at the same hotel and in the same room." We both turned to look at each other at the same time. "What a coincidence don't you think?" She said. "It is strange. Feels like you were leading us here. Were you guiding us to this place Frank?"

I'm not sure how to respond to her question. She only knows the old me. How is she going to react to this Deacon Frank Mosley? Stacy has never been inside a church. Not even to the funeral of a family member. "Stacy you never told me how you located where I lived."

"I only knew about the church from Facebook, so we parked outside and waited until you came out. I didn't recognize you at first with the facial hair, but that walk, only you strolled like that. We followed you to your place, and I waited a few days until I got up enough nerve to knock on the door."

"Glad you both are here. Speaking of the church, I need to share something with you. I started going when I first got here. I was skeptical at first because you know I wasn't into the church scene. Then one night during a revival, I gave my life to God. I'm a Deacon now. I teach Wednesday's Bible study, Sunday school and occasionally preach when the pastor asks."

"That would explain the way you are dress along with the different tone in you conversation. I can't promise I'll go with you to church. I'm the same street chick you met back home. Not to up on religious folks. I'm more of your club and Hennessey kind of girl.

"I don't expect for you to change overnight. Just consider our daughter in your decision making. If you would, at least attend a few services with me."

"You truly have changed. I'll go to your church only because I want to see what females are pushing up on my man."

"There she is. I was wondering when the real Stacy Cherry was going to show up. You don't need to come with any drama. I came here single and I'm still single. Now please let's go in here to get your stuff." I replied.

I got out and went around to open her door. She gets out with her lips poked out. She pushed me out the way then took Gabrielle out her car seat. "Can I get the room key please?" She just throws them at me. I opened the door to find the room a mess. Stacy has never been known for her cleanliness.

"Don't even start Frank, I can see you about to open your mouth. Just help me pack please."

"I'm not going to comment on this room. As far as my place, if you plan to live with me, then this is not going to work. You already know how I feel about a dirty crib. Now let's go to the front desk so we can pay the bill."

We put the bags in the car then drove around to the front to check out. Being I have two more mouths to feed, we went over to Walmart. As we entered the store, I already noticed people from the church checking Stacy and Gabrielle out. I just kept her attention much as possible. The last thing I need is for her to show her behind in the store. We managed to get our shopping done and check out without a confrontation. We drove back over to my place. After I had put the money in a safe place, I helped Stacy fix dinner.

"Look at us Frank, a nice happy family. I didn't think this day would ever come. After the way you dismissed me on that rooftop, I just knew I would be another black single mother."

"About that night, I never meant a word of it. I just didn't want you getting caught up in my mess. I didn't have time to watch your back and mine. The dudes I was dealing with were too dangerous. Looks like it didn't work out that way. Please never talk about being a single mother, you of all people seen what my mom went through. I will never be the father mine was to me. My child will know the love of a real man, and I will show and teach her how she should be treated. That way no one can come to her with any kind of foolishness."

She started kissing my neck. "Girl, you need to stop before we burn the food."

"Frank you know it's been so long. I have been faithful all this time even when you were locked down." Why she got to bring that up. She is not going to like this next part.

"Look Stacy, before you get upset, just hear me out ok," I said while moving backward.

"What Frank? You always killing my groove with something."

"Being that I live a Christian life now, there will be no sex before marriage."

"See, I would be going off right now, but you said Marriage so I can't even get upset with you. So when are we getting married tomorrow?"

"Slow your roll sweetheart. We need to get this other business straighten out first then we need to go through premarital counseling with

Pastor Walker first. After that, we can set a date." She didn't like that too much, but she didn't disagree. I set the table so we could eat. As we were sitting down at the table, Stacy was about to start eating. "Wait a minute Stacy!" I yelled out.

"What? Did I do something?" She asked.

I scared Gabrielle when I yelled out. I picked her up and placed her on my lap. "No you didn't do anything wrong. In this house, every meal is blessed before eaten."

"This new you is going to take some time for me to adjust too. Please do your thing and bless our first meal together," She said with a smile on her face.

"Father, we come before you thanking you for what you have provided. We thank you for allowing this family unit to be made whole again, and for the new addition that is truly a blessing. In your name, we pray, Amen." I lifted my eyes to see Stacy wiping tears from her own eyes.

"I'm sorry for crying. I never heard you pray before, and to be doing it while holding your child, priceless. Now let's eat before the food gets cold."

We both glance over at each between bites. I wonder what's running through her mind right now. Seeing the new me has got to be a shock. I just hope she can adjust to my lifestyle. I know how much she loves the club scene, drinking and smoking weed. None of that will be going on around my child. Of course I need to be opened minded. I have not been around her for over a year, and she may have changed.

After we had got done, I cleaned the dishes. We then went for a walk around the block. Once back in the apartment, she gave Gabrielle a bath while I sat watching the basketball game. When she was done laying her down to sleep, she joined me on the couch.

"So how you feel about this town?" She asked.

"It's sure not Detroit, but the people here are so friendly," I replied.

"Why did you pick this place?"

"I didn't pick it, it picked me. My car broke down here, and my life has been better since that day."

"What are the sleeping arrangements sweetheart," She asked.

"I'm sleeping on the sofa while you and Gabrielle take the bedroom."

"What, you're not sleeping with me? Is that part of this no sex before marriage?"

"Yes. I need to respect my child. She's old enough to start understanding what's going on around her. It kills me how parents fool themselves thinking their kids don't know what they see. They soak up everything like a sponge, and it's up to us to show them right from wrong. Most little kids can sing a whole rap song with explicit lyrics, but can't hardly do the basic things they should know.

The Bible says, "We perish from a lack of knowledge." I should know firsthand because I was on the road to failure. I thought I knew it all when I learned how to hustle. Only hustling I was doing was straight to an early grave. Ask me anything about that life, I could spit it off my tongue. Ask me about credit scores, saving accounts, balancing a check book, stocks, bonds, interest rates, home loans, applying for college, Etc. I would look at you like you were crazy."

"Frank that was deep. You made me think about my life right then. I didn't think anything of it when I played my rap CD's while Gabrielle was in the car. Or when I lite up around her. She is starting to try and sing the words I noticed. My mindset was she's too young to know better. I see now that was wrong. Are you mad at me?"

"Of course not. We don't know we are doing wrong unless we learn what is right. What's that old saying, two wrongs don't make it right? I guess one of us had to come out of the darkness to see it was wrong. Now together we can move forward nor backwards."

"That sounds good to me. I'm ready to see more of this new life you have. Not saying I'm all in on going to church yet. You know how I feel about that," She replied.

Just to hear her say that, was good enough for me. We sat and talked way into the night until our eyes couldn't stay open. I gave her a hug before going into the room to give my baby girl a kiss goodnight. I showed Stacy where everything was before going to sleep on the sofa. This day has been a day fill with blessings. I can't wait to see what tomorrow brings.

*************

The next morning, I made sure to tip around not to wake them up. I took a shower and grabbed a cup of coffee before heading to work. I left Stacy a note because I never got around to telling her where I worked. I took the money with me, I need to figure what to do with it. I counted it out while she was sleep. It was around $150,000. She kept everything I put away. She was correct when she said she was down for me. Anyone else would have disappeared with that kind of loot. I didn't owe but $10,000 to my old connect. I'll make arrangements to square away that debt. They won't stop looking for me until they get their money. The rest is still drug money so I need to choose my decision carefully. I can't give the money back so that makes it hard. I broke it up in stacks of ten's which made it easier to stash in my car. A good day's work will keep my mind occupied.

"Good Morning Jake, how is it going this fine day?"

"Well, you seem to be all Chipper this today. What gives?"

"Jake, I received the best gift anyone could want," I said.

He was standing there just looking at me waiting to hear everything.

"What you won the lottery, and come to tell me you're quitting?"

"No. I found out I'm a father. I have a daughter name Gabrielle who will be turning two soon. I'm the happiest father alive," I replied sounding excited.

"That's great news Frank. Where is she, back home in Detroit with her mother?"

"No. They are both back at my place sleep. They showed up at my door yesterday after church. I was like a deer in headlights when I opened the front door."

"I'm so happy for you. What are you going to do now, and will wedding bells be coming up soon?"

"We talked about it, but not until we go through premarital counseling with the pastor.

"How is she taking you being into the church also a Deacon?"

"She's cool with it. Least that's what she said. I know it's going to be a struggle to adjust from her old lifestyle at first. I don't want to push her to attend church or beat her up with scriptures. I'll just let her see God through my lifestyle."

"Frank you are wise beyond your years. You actually have come a long way from the time you rolled into town," He replied.

I told him a little more about Stacy and Gabrielle then we got to work. I didn't tell him about the money. I figure the less he knows about it, the better. I worked at a quicker paced than normal. I wanted to get back home to my family. Did I just say that? I was about to head to lunch when Jake came running over to my car. "Wait up a second Frank, I need to talk with you."

"What's up Jake? It's after 12:00." I stepped out of the car to see what was so important.

"Look, come on in the office. I'll order us a pizza for lunch. I want to go over something with you."

"Jake, I was going to the house to have lunch with my family. What's that important it can't wait until I get back?" I said.

He didn't say a word, just started walking to the office. I know Jake, if he's like this, then let me see what he wants. I followed behind him.

"Have a seat Frank," He told me.

"You sure nothing is wrong Jake? You sure are acting funny."

"Frank, I had this on my mind for a while now. After your good news you shared, and I can see how proud it made you feel, I don't see the need to wait any longer. I just need you to sign these papers right here, here, and here."

"Jake what is this?" I couldn't believe what I was reading.

"Frank, I'm making you part owner of my business. With your new responsibility as a family man, your current salary won't pay the bills. You have proven more than capable of running things around here. Well, what do you say Frank?"

"I don't know what to say. It's your life's work Jake. You sure you want to give away half of it to someone your barely know?"

"Would you quit talking and sign the papers already. I have complete confidence it's right for both of us. I haven't known you that long, but with all we been through, it makes up for years," He said.

We both fell out laughing when I realized what he meant. I took my time going over each document because it was a business transaction. I'm not too up on how it goes, but I trust Jake not to screw me over. I said a quick prayer to myself then signed all the papers.

"Now was that so hard? Welcome to the salvage yard business partner."

"I just hope I don't let you down. You have been like a father in a funny kind of way which means a lot to me. I can't wait to go home and tell Stacy what happen."

"Well, now that we got that out of the way, how about we tear into this pizza then get back to making money. You should know my slogan my now." He's right, I sure did. "Time is money." We enjoyed our food then headed back out when we heard a customer blowing the horn. I told Jake I'll take care of it while he just stood by and watched. It was my first time dealing with a customer. Any other time I was out back doing whatever. When the customer left, he called me over. "What up Jake?" Sounding worried. "Why don't you head on home to the family. I know you want to get back to them."

"I sure appreciate that. I'll see you in the morning." I headed back into the office to get my things.

# Kerry

Frank been avoiding my phone calls. Wonder what's going on with him. Let me just stop by his apartment to see for myself. I know we said we would stay in the friend zone, but something keeps pulling me to him. Don't know if it's because of that night he saved my life. It doesn't matter the reason, all I know is I think I love him. Let me run through the drive-thru at Starbucks to get a cup of coffee first.

"Welcome to Starbucks, are you ready to order?" A voice said from the speaker.

"Yes. Give me a large Latte, please," I said before pulling up to the window for my total.

"Here you go. Hello First Lady Walker," She said.

Shoot, I forgot my husband's niece worked here. Need to think of something quick.

"Hey sweetie, how is your mother?" I said. I didn't really want to know. I was trying to be polite.

"She is doing fine. I'll tell her you asked about her," She replied.

"You do that. Bye, bye now," I said before driving off.

Now I have to make this quick; I'm supposed to be heading home to cook dinner. When she lets her mother know she saw me, that heifer going to call Henry. She can't stand me either. I don't see his car parked outside. Let me just knock away. Maybe he's having car trouble.

"Well, hello who might you be? Frank didn't say anything about he had family coming into town."

"I need to be asking you that same thing! I'm his fiancée."

Who is this woman in my man's apartment? He has some explaining to do. I couldn't do anything but stare this little thing down. She was looking like one of them rap video girls.

"I'm a good friend of Frank's, and we are very, very, close. Please tell him I stopped by to see him, please."

"You don't have to worry about that; that's not all I'm going to be telling him. Now if you can get yourself out of my doorway before we have a problem!!!"

"I can see you don't come from much class so I will excuse myself. Bye now." I didn't even give her a chance to respond. I should have thrown this coffee in her face."

**********************

## Stacy

Who was that woman? She got some nerve coming around here. She doesn't know; I'm straight up from the hood. I should have dragged her high mighty behind out there on that sidewalk. Oh, I'm so mad right now I could... "Mommy, are you ok. Why are you yelling?"

"Come here baby girl, mommy is so sorry you had to hear that. I hate you had to see me like that. One of daddy's friends made me mad." I forgot Gabrielle was playing in the bedroom. When that man walks through that door, I may catch a charge.

"Hello family, I'm so glad to be home."

He tried to give me a kiss on the cheek, but I was not feeling that right now.

"What's got your face bent out of shape now Stacy?"

"You should ask your girlfriend you don't have!"

"First thing, lower your voice around my daughter. Second thing, what are you talking about?"

"Let me put her in the other room," I said.

I took Gabrielle back into the bedroom then closed the door so she couldn't hear.

"Could you please tell me why you are so upset?" He asked

"Some high-class chick came over here looking for you. She made sure to emphasize, she knew you very well. Frank, you know I will slice a chick quick."

"That had to be Kerry; she is the pastor's wife. She means nothing to me outside of the church. She must of stop by for Church business. She can rub you wrong if you don't know her. I'm sorry she made you upset."

I know it's more to it than that, but I'll let it go for now. "That's fine; you just need to let her know she's not welcome here."

"I will take care of it first thing in the morning. Can we please talk about something else now?" He said.

I didn't even responded to his statement, I just walked into the kitchen to start dinner.

***********

## Pastor Walker

So glad to be home after spending a few hours at the nursing home praying for the sick and shut-in. Where is that wife of mine now? She should have beat me home an hour ago. Can't she even take Sunday off from creeping? Lord, please forgive me for my remark. I'm just tired of her mess. I know you said to keep her in prayer, but when am I going to see the results of that praying? I'm not questioning you, just talking out loud. Wait I can hear her car pulling into the garage. Thank you Lord for bringing her home, speak to you later.

"Kerry, where have you been? You should have been home a half hour ago.

"Please don't start bombarding me with questions. I made a quick stop to see a friend. Do I need to get your permission in everything I do?"

"I'm tired of having to keep up a façade about our marriage in front of people."

"Well, you don't have to remember. You yelled it out for all the world to hear, "I knew all the time!!" Did I get it right?"

"I just can't with you right now. I'm going to fix me something to eat."

She followed right behind me into the kitchen still talking. "Where you think you're going? You started this so let's finish. If you that tired of playing house, why don't you just divorce me?"

"Kerry, you know I will never divorce you. I'm a man of God; we are used to battles with the devil. So get that out your beautiful little head. Now if you will excuse me, I like to be alone right now. I picked up an apple off the counter then walked out without making eye contact.

"You can preach about communication, but you can't do it in your own home. I'm going for a drive to clear my head, and don't try and stop me either."

## Kerry

I grabbed my car keys and headed for the garage hoping he would stop me. After getting into my car, I sat there for a few minutes. When I accepted he wasn't coming, I reached down in my purse getting my cell phone to call Kelly.

"Hello Kelly, are you busy right now. I need to come over?"

"Kerry, why are you crying? Of course you can come over." She said sounding worried.

"Henry and I had another fight when I came home."

"Don't say another word, get yourself over here." She hung up on me. I know she's tired of hearing about our problems. I got my face together then headed over to her house. "Thanks for letting me come over Kelly. Where is Rodney?"

"He's over at the office getting things together for an open house coming up. Come on into the living room." I followed her into the living room and took a seat on the sofa. "So what happen this time? On the outside you both look like the perfect couple. On the inside, you both are a train wreck."

"I went by to see Frank before going home that's all. When I got home, He went off on me." She gave me that look of not him again.

"When are you going to leave that man to live his life?"

"I may have no choice now. Some girl answered the door looking like a hood rat. She called herself trying to intimidate me. I was going to throw my coffee on her. "My God, would you look at yourself Kerry. This man is not your husband!!! Pastor Henry Walker is your husband!!! Look, I can't do this with you. Please leave now!!! Please leave my house." She got up pulling me toward the front door. Without even a goodbye, she slammed the door in my face. I was going to knock, but I'll let her settle back down. I went back home to face whatever he was going to do.

# Kelly

That was too close. Where are my pills? I took two then went upstairs to lie down on my bed.

"Honey, I'm home. Where are you?"

Lord, I was hoping the pills would kick in before he came back. I'm too weak to call out to him.

"You in the bed early, everything ok?" He said checking for a fever with his hand.

"Yes. I'm just a little tired that's all. Nothing to worry about."

"Kelly, I saw Kerry leaving as I drove up. She upset you; I can see it in your eyes. When are you going to tell her that your cancer has spread? I don't need you wasting your strength on her foolishness. I love you, and I need you around long as the Lord will allow."

"I'm sorry. I tried to tell her last time she was here, but she's so fixated on Deacon Mosley nothing else matters," I explained.

I can see Rodney was getting upset. This man loves me so much; I need to consider his feeling in all this. I come to terms that my days is numbered. Kerry's house may be going through hell, but I want to leave my house in peace. "Honey please forgive me for not putting your needs first. God comes first in my life; then it's my husband. I won't forget that again."

"So what happen to her crazy self this time?"

"She went over to Frank's apartment today, and got a rude awakening when his girlfriend answered the door."

"I would have paid anything to see the look on her face. You would think she stopped all that running around after almost getting killed."

"Maybe it's going to take God himself to wake her up out of the fantasy."

"Well enough about her. Let's get you back to bed so you can rest, please."

# Rodney

After I had put Kelly back in bed, I went back downstairs. I went into the basement so she couldn't hear me cry. I started beating the punching bag I had hung up in the corner. I know they say a man shouldn't cry, but when your emotions build up, you need to release so you can think better. Seeing her like that hurt my heart so much.

Lord, I would never second guess your will in my life, but I can't wrap my head around as to why you let my wife get cancer. You placed me in the right place at the right time to stop her from jumping off that bridge. I was supposed to be doing an open house that day. For some reason, I left the welcome sign in the garage and had to turn back around. When I took one look into her eyes, I didn't see color. All I saw was the woman I wanted to spend the rest of my life married too. Some people call it love at first sight. We called it "love at the first jump." Not making lite of the situation, we just choose to find the positive out of a negative. If I could trade places with her, I would in a second. Even when she told me about what happen with her Uncle, my love for her never wavered. If anything, it became stronger for her. We often bring up children in our lives. I always wanted a son of my own. When the doctor told us it would be too risky, I wasn't going to be selfish. We both have come to terms and found peace with it. Well, let me get back upstairs. Nice talking with you Lord as always. "Honey, I was just about to come down and get you. What were you doing?"

"I was having some alone time with the Lord in the basement."

"That's what I love about you. You will converse with God, and not let things build up to the point where anger takes over. Now hurry up and take a shower and come to bed. My feet are cold as ice, and I need some snuggle time with my husband."

# Kerry

I know Rodney saw me driving away when he pulled up. He is going to blame me for upsetting Kelly. She was the one who threw me out without an explanation. Maybe they are having trouble in their marriage that she doesn't want me to know. Who am I kidding? She has a great marriage unlike mine which is a mess. It's times like this when I would get with one of my male admirers to take my mind off my troubles.

Tonight, I'm not even feeling that. I have been driving around for half an hour now. It's time I go home and face the music away. When I pulled up into the driveway, I could see the light in his office was still on. I wonder what he is talking about with God now. Don't take a rocket scientist to know it's me. Let's see if I can make it to the bedroom without being lectured to death. I just wish for once he would talk to me like a husband and not as a preacher. When we first met, I didn't have to guess how he felt about me. Now it's almost like I'm competing with his Bible for attention. Everything is a scripture whenever we have a conversation. I guess my running around with men doesn't help the matter either. Well here we go again. I opened the door quietly as I could, but these stupid motion sensors gave me away. He said they were put in because of the crime in the area, but I know it was to alert him when I tried to seek in the house. He put them in right after he found the stash of lingerie I kept hidden in the laundry room.

"Hello Honey, welcome back home. Did you have a nice visit with Kelly?"

"How did you know I was with her tonight? I didn't tell you where I was going."

"She called to see if you made it home safely. I was worried also when you left. I don't want to fuss with you. Can we just go to bed, and see how we feel in the morning?"

"That will please me more than anything right now." He walked over and placed a soft kiss on my lips before returning to his office. I went up to our bedroom and went to bed.

## Pastor Walker

Lord, Thank you for giving me an abundant amount of Christian patience. Because if I was still in the world married to this woman, I would be on the first thing smoking. She thinks I'm in here all time in my Bible. She is correct, but if she only knew the real reason as to why. Being a Pastor comes with a great deal of responsibility, one being trust. When her sister and husband first came to me with her diagnosis of lung cancer three years ago, I been in constant prayer. Now they come to me with her lung cancer has spread, and the doctors gave her a prognosis of fewer than six months. They asked me not to share this information with anyone including Kerry. Good or bad she is still my wife. I don't feel comfortable with this, but as a Pastor, I have to respect their decision through the process. I'm still standing on God's word for complete healing. It says in Isaiah 53:5, **"But he was wounded for our transgressions, he was bruised for our iniquities: the chastisement of our peace was him; and**

**with his stripes we are healed."** I could break out in a praise right now. After another hour of praying, I went to see what Kerry was doing. I found her on her knees praying. I just stood in the doorway until she was done.

"What you standing in the doorway watching me for?"

"I can't watch my wife praying to the Lord? You look so peaceful in that position."

"Who said I was praying? I dropped one of my earrings; it rolled under the bed."

I just smiled as I pulled some pajamas from the chester drawer before going into the bathroom. When I came out, Kerry was in bed reading one of her beauty magazines.

"You mind if I turn the lights off, I have an early meeting in the morning."

"You pay the bills so I guess you can do whatever you want with them." I didn't even entertain her sarcastic remark with a reply. Lord just get me through the night, please.

# Frank

I didn't wake Stacy from her sleep. I took a shower then left. I wanted to get to work early, that way I can take an early lunch. My plan was to meet with Kerry later today and put a stop to her coming to my place. She may think she is all that, but she hasn't seen a bad day until Stacy goes to her behind. Good, that scrap truck hasn't pulled up yet. I can least eat my bacon, egg, and cheese biscuit before I get started. Just soon as I was about to take a bite, I heard the driver blowing his horn. I wrapped it back up and placed it back in the bag before heading out the door.

"You can go back to eating your breakfast; I'll take care of this."

"How you beat me here Jake?" I didn't even see his truck when I pulled up."

"I get up way before the crack of dawn. I can't make money resting on my buns."

"You're right about that. Let me give you a hand so we can get this guy out of here."

I put my gloves on to give the driver a hand. When we were finished, I followed Jake back into the office.

"Jake, you mind if I take off a little early today."

"Of course not. What you got going on if you don't mind me asking?"

"I know you know me and Kerry had a thing going on. Well she showed up at my house yesterday. Stacy answered the door and let's just say it didn't go to good. So I plan on talking to Kerry face to face today."

"I'm not going to tell you what to do. Just be careful with that one. She has proven to make a volcano look tame." I busted out laughing.

"Yes she can Jake, but I have her match right at home. I'm not trying to see them two collide either."

He reminded me that I was a partner, and I didn't need to ask for permission to leave early anymore. I worked until around 11:30 before heading to meet with Kerry. I had already called her which she agreed to the meeting. We met at Hal & Kathy's Cook House which was a popular place on Main St. It didn't matter now when people saw us together. I greeted several people as I made my way to the table where she was waiting.

"Hello Kerry, Thank you for meeting with me."

"So what's so important that I get the pleasure of you company? Don't think I didn't notice how you picked this place so I won't show out. Let's just see how that works out for you."

"Look, I didn't come here for all that noise. I just want you to understand that I won't allow you to cause problems between my fiancée and me."

"So that is who the little hood rat was. I'm so happy for you both."

"Kerry, don't ever let me hear you come out your mouth in a disrespectful manner toward Stacy in my presence again."

"Or what Deacon Frank Mosley? Remember you gave that life up to follow God."

"Yes I did, but I been studying up on backsliding. You should be very familiar with that in your lifestyle. You already know my history so don't make me have a flashback."

We both sat there staring each other down like it was a nuclear weapons standoff. I could see her cheeks puffing up with rage while rolling her eyes almost in the back of her head. I was waiting for the top of head to pop off like a pressure cooker.

"Well Kerry, do we understanding one another?"

"Fine, I won't cause any problems for you and what's her name. Anything else?"

"I think that will do it for now. You enjoy your lunch First Lady Walker."

I left knowing she was full of crap, and she needs time to contemplate her next move. I left there and went through McDonalds drive thru. Dealing with her, I forgot to order something to eat. From there, I made my way home to hug my little princess. That little girl has brought so much joy into my life. Soon as I opened the front door, Gabrielle ran into my arms. I couldn't help but to shed a tear. It wasn't because she was in my arms. It was for wanting my mother to be able to have the same experience. Then again I wouldn't want Gabrielle to see her grandmother in that condition.

"Hey, I didn't hear you come in. how was your day at work?"

"It was good. I only worked until around 11:30." I wasn't going to start off this new relationship lying to her.

"So in that case, where have you been this whole time?" I can see she was getting upset. Stacy can go from 0 to 100 real quick without warning. "Calm yourself down and let me explain, please."

"Frank, you better not be cheating on me. I didn't come to California for no games."

"Is not even like that sweetie. I had a conversation with Kerry; I told her I wasn't going to allow her psychotic self to mess up what we have."

"Frank, I don't need you standing up for me. Have you been gone from the streets that long where you forgot that we handle our own beef? I forgot you preaching that love thy neighbor stuff now. Where I'm from, your neighbor comes at you wrong then you beat that behind."

"I don't know who is worst, you or Kerry. In this house, there is only the peace of God. Do you understand that?" She gets up from the sofa and goes into the bedroom.

"Let me share this with you, you got your peace of God, and I got my piece right here. My chrome plated 9mm locked and loaded." She yelled out.

"Where in the world did you get that gun from?" I shouted while taking it from her hand.

"Stop tripping. You didn't think I was rolling and not be strapped. Frank, you can't expect for me to change just because I came to this place. Did you change overnight when you got here?"

She did have a point about changing. I couldn't see my faults until I came against something stronger than me. It was not done with force, instead with love and grace.

"You know Stacy, you are right. I can't expect for you just to walk away from all that you ever knew without showing something better to replace it. Why don't you come to our Wednesday night Bible study?" If not for yourself, then do it for our child. Give her a chance to know something other than what she has already seen. That way when she's older, she can make her own decision."

"I'm not dressing up or carrying no Bible. If you agree to that, then I will go," She said.

I didn't respond to what she said. I walked over and took her into my arms. For Stacy to agree to go to church, words couldn't do it justice. "Now where is daddy's little blessing."

"Frank, don't go waking that child up. I just got her down for a nap."

"She can sleep when we get back. Right now I want to take my two ladies to the park."

"That will be great because I'm tired of being in the house. I'll get her ready."

While she did that, I took a quick wash up in the bathroom. This one bedroom apartment was good enough for just me, but it is not adequate for the three of us. I need to find a better place for us soon.

"You coming out that bathroom anytime today Frank?" She called out.

"Yeah, sooner the better," I replied.

I opened the door placing a soft kiss on Stacy's neck as she pushed passed me. I went back into the living room until they were ready.

"Ok, here is your little blessing." Gabrielle ran into my arms giving me the biggest hug. "Daddy! Daddy! Mommy said you were taking us to the park."

"That's right baby girl. Now put your shoes on so we can go."

After she had got her shoes on, we headed to the car. I drove them to the park on the other side of town because the equipment was better than what we had over here. I don't care where you live; you will always have the haves and the haves-nots neighborhoods. It's sad how a few blocks can make a big difference. Watching Stacy facial expressions, I can see even she noticed the drastic difference. After I parked the car, I went around to help Gabrielle out of her car seat.

"Daddy, I want to get on the sliding board," She asked.

I told her to let me get her out the car first. We ran over to the play area as fast as her little feet would go. She slid down a few times until she caught a glimpse of the swings.

"Daddy! Daddy! Come on and push me," She shouted.

"Anything for my little blessing. Come on and I'll carry you over to them."

I placed her in the middle swing because other white children were occupying the other ones. As I was pushing her, I looked over and noticed Stacy looking like she was ready to leave. I picked up Gabrielle and walked over to see what was wrong.

"Why the long face sweetheart?" I asked.

"Frank, what are we doing here? Look at this place and these people, we don't belong here at all. We are from the streets. At least that's where I come from. I don't even recognize you anymore. Can we please just get out of here?"

I have seen her stand down someone with a gun in her face without batting an eye, but this was totally not the same person. I picked up Gabrielle; Stacy was already halfway to the car. After putting her in her car seat, I tried to give Stacy a kiss but she just turned away. Her eyes were fixed out her window. I'm worried about her. I didn't notice the Pearl Black Chrysler 300 tailing us until about three blocks. I know that car from somewhere. I took a couple of quick turns to see if they would follow us. They turned off one block back; maybe it was just my imagination playing tricks with my mind. We made it back to the apartment still without communicating. I went around to get Gabrielle.

"Daddy, what's wrong with mommy?" She asked.

I looked up where Stacy was seated; I saw a single tear fall from her left eye. Right then I knew if I couldn't reach her heart soon; I would come home and she would be gone.

"Mommy's alright sweetie, she just had something in her eye."

Stacy got out going straight into the apartment. Sometimes in life situations, all you can do is pray. Definitely, this is one of those times where I will be praying.

Wednesday night had finally gotten here; I was glad because it was time for Bible study.

"Honey you and Gabrielle ready to go?" I called out.

"Yes. Just let me finish doing her hair. You sure I look alright for your church friends?" After spending two hours convincing her what she had on was fine, she went and changed again. "For the last time, you look great. Now can we please make our way to the car?"

"I'm just nervous about going that's all. Let me get a sweater to cover up my tattoos first."

"Will you just come on? It's too hot outside to be wearing a sweater. Nobody is going to judge you," I explained.

I think God is the only one I seen who could get her this nervous. We made it over to the church just before service started. As we walked inside, of course all eyes were on us. Only a few people knew that Stacy and Gabrielle were in town. I felt with everything that had occurred with Kerry and James, I didn't want to expose her to a lot of questions. Plus everyone knows how church folks can get in your business.

"Well, good evening Deacon Mosley. Who is this lovely woman, and this precious little one?

"Good evening Mother Mary. This is my fiancée Stacy, and this little one is my daughter Gabrielle. They moved here to live with me."

"Well looks like you been a busy man. When you get engaged? I can't believe you kept this from me."

"It not what you think Mother. We recently got engaged after she got here. I didn't even know about my daughter until I saw her for the first time. You know I would never disrespect you like that."

"That's good to hear. Well service is starting, but we will finish our conversation later."

We went inside and took seats in the back. I didn't want to give Stacy too much of an uncomfortable feeling being it was her first time.

"Frank who was that old lady? She sure likes to talk," She said laughing.

"That was Mother Mary; she is one of the mothers of the church. She has played a vital role in my life since I been living here. You can safely say, that if not for God and her I would not be sitting here today."

"What in the heck is a mother of the church?"

I couldn't help but laugh when she said that. I knew I would have to explain a lot of things about the church to them both. I passed her a note explaining the role of the church mother. After reading it, she drew a happy face then sat back to listen to the service. Right before service was over, I led them both out to the lobby.

"Is everything ok Frank? Why are we leaving early?" She asked.

"I thought maybe you wanted to leave service early so you didn't have to answer any more questions."

"I appreciate your concern, but I was enjoying what he was saying. He was dropping some deep stuff. This church thing may not be as bad as I thought. I been listening to other people bad mouth God for so many years, I just didn't want any part of it. I guess the best thing is to come judge for yourself."

"Look at you, I didn't see this coming. Do you feel up to meeting some of the members?"

"I don't see why not. I'm going to have to face them sometimes."

Just when she said that, I saw Kerry and Pastor walking towards us.

"Well, I finally get to meet the women in Deacon's life. I heard you both were in town. This is my wife First Lady Walker," Pastor Walker said.

I could tell by Kerry's face balling up; she didn't know about Gabrielle.

"It's good to meet you Pastor Walker. Frank speaks highly of you."

If looks could kill, I would be dead the way Kerry is staring at me.

"Honey if you will excuse me, I need to go to the restroom," Kerry said.

Kerry turns and walks off. Judging by her body motion, that was one upset sister. I just hope she doesn't break anything in the bathroom. Hopefully she won't forget that she is in the house of the Lord. I could also feel that Pastor Walker knew she had a problem with Stacy being here. I often ask myself how he doesn't know about our affair. Maybe he knows but doesn't want to believe it. Whatever the case, I'm okay with keeping it in the past.

********************

# Kerry

I went into the bathroom slamming the door while throwing my purse on the counter. Looking into the mirror with my eyeliner about to run down my cheeks, I had promised myself I wouldn't cry over that man again. That little girl is his daughter? I didn't see her the day I went over to his place. When? How? Why? All these things are running through my head right now.

I slammed my hand down, chipping three of my manicured nails. Shoot, I just had them done yesterday. Frank, how could you do this to me? He is still hiding secrets from his past life. Look at me talking about him like he is my man. Why am I talking to myself in the bathroom mirror is the biggest question. Let me fix my face and get out of here. As I was applying my makeup, I heard the door opening. "Oh, it's just you. What can I do for you?"

"Look Kerry, I could see you were having some kind of moment out there. I'm just here to clear the air female to female. I had my suspicious about you and Frank from the minute you knocked on my door. You walking away like that just confirmed it. You should know as a woman; you never tip your hand by showing your emotions."

"You're correct about your suspicious, but we don't have anything going on anymore. That had ended before you came to town."

"Then why you in here all caught up in your feelings?"

"When I saw your daughter for the first time, it was hard to accept. Frank never mentioned anything about her."

"That's because he didn't know. I just told him when I came to town. He was just as surprised as you were. I hope this is not going to cause you to do anything you will regret in the future."

"That sounded like a threat if I'm not mistaken, but don't get me twisted. I may not be from the hood, but I can hold my own."

"Trust and believe you little rich chick, mess with my family and you will come up missing. I promised Frank, I would give this place a try without acting up. In your case, I will make an exception." We both stood there trying to intimidate one another like we were in high school. "Look hood rat, I don't have time to stand here with you. I have better things to do with my valuable time. Now if you move out my way, I would like to rejoin my husband."

Before I knew it, she was in my face breathing hard. "My name is Stacy for the last time!!" She shouted. I pushed her off then ran out the door; I didn't even look back to see if she was behind me. I walked back over to where my husband was still talking to Frank. "I didn't think you were ever coming out of that bathroom honey."

"Sorry it took so long. We were just having a little girl talk. So are you ready to go?" I didn't wait for his reply before heading toward the exit. I wasn't about to deal with miss thing another minute."

"What in the world are you in such a hurry for?" He asked.

"There is something wrong with Frank's little friend. She must be on drugs."

"Why do you say that? She seems to be friendly enough. What happen in the bathroom?"

"She just comes off in the wrong tone that's all. I don't see her fitting in around here at all."

"Well, I say we give her the same chance we gave Frank when he came to town. You didn't say that about him. You took a liking to him right away."

"You're right. I guess I can do that. Let's just hope the Lord doesn't take too long reaching her. This town can't take another round like before. I know I sure can't deal with it." I had to cut the conversation short before he starts asking too many questions. I just reached over and turned the CD player on so he wouldn't talk anymore. Now that's better so I can think. What am I going to do about this situation? Don't think for one minute I'm going to allow that little miss ghetto girl to come into town and run things. There is only one Queen of Fall River Mills and that would be me. I pulled down the sun visor so I could see myself in the mirror. Looking into my own eyes, I could see the other Kerry staring back. No matter what I did, she won't leave. In some ways, I like her being around.

Look at him over there with that dumb expression on his face. He takes to Frank like a son and has no idea how many times I spent in his bed. How could he be a man of God and can't even discern the infidelity that's has taken place right under his nose. Maybe I did so much that his brain is in overload. Whatever it is, I can say he is rooted and grounded in the Lord. The average man couldn't even weather a storm with me. I would just chew them up and spit them out like sour candy. Enough of that, let me get back to what I was thinking. Oh yes, little Miss ghetto girl.

## Frank

"What is taking her so long?" I was thinking to myself as I was trying to chase after Gabrielle who was running all around the lobby. Just when I was picking her up, I see Stacy coming out of the restroom. She has that look on her face as if someone peed in her cornflakes.

"What's wrong with you sweetheart? Did she say something to you?"

"Come on let's get to the car before I have to curse in this place."

Something told me this was going to be a long ride back home. I made a conscious decision to let her drive hoping it would keep her from doing anything with Gabrielle in the car. I knew whatever it was involved Kerry and that is never a good thing.

"You think you're slick by letting me drive, but it's cool for now. Wait till we get to the crib, I got a few choice words for your behind. Going try to play me for a fool. You picked the wrong one this time!"

I sat there with my mouth shut until I found out exactly what happen in that bathroom. While keeping my eyes staring out my window to avoid further backlash, I noticed that same pearl black Chrysler 300 following behind us in the passenger side mirror. It was nighttime, but there is no mistaking those headlights. It didn't turn off till we were just about to the house. Who is this person and what do they want? Maybe I'm thinking too much into this. There are a lot of nice rides in this town. Either way; I'm moving us to a safer spot next week.

I wasn't going to let nothing happen to my family even if it cost me my life. I turned around to see how Gabrielle was doing because she was so quiet. I couldn't help but smile when I saw how peaceful she looked sleeping. The look on her face was the way I wanted my life to be at this stage of my life. Just seems to be forces that are getting ready for another battle against me.

Well devil if you're coming, you better bring more then you brought last time. When we pulled up, Stacy got out then took Gabrielle before going into the house. When I went inside, she was in the bedroom with the door closed. I just got a blanket, and went to sleep on the couch. There was no need to keep adding fuel to the fire.

**\*\*\*\*\*\*\*\***

# Frank

A few weeks had gone by without us having many long conversations. I was able to find a bigger house on the nicer side of town. On my way back to the apartment with the moving truck, I spotted Officer Jones coming out of a convenience store. Pulled in while blowing the horn to get his attention.

"What's up Deacon Mosley, how are things going with you?"

"Glad you asked. Do you know of anyone who owns a pearl black Chrysler 300?"

"Can't say that I do right off hand. You having a problem with someone?"

"Not that I know of Jones. Well, I must be going now. See you later."

"Wait for a second Frank. You would tell me if there is a problem in my town wouldn't you? I don't want the same chain of events like before."

We just stood there looking at each other. Should I tell him about the money Stacy brought with her? He already knows about my dealings with the Drug connect and my history in Detroit. I still need more time to check things out for myself. "Of course I would tell you if anything was going on. If you can't trust the police, then who can you trust?"

"I'll hold you to that Frank. Look I have a meeting to get to, so I'll check you out later."

I didn't think he was working today being dressed in plain clothes. When I pulled up in front of the apartment blowing the horn, I could see Stacy peeking through the mini blinds. I didn't know who was worse her or Gabrielle. In a matter of weeks they had my blinds looking like they were two years old.

"What are you doing home with this moving truck?"

"Now you want to talk to me? If you must know, we are moving so start packing, please."

"Where are we moving to Frank? I am not touching a thing until you tell me."

"Look, I know you're mad about something that happened way before you got here. Just trust that I'm doing the best thing for my family right now."

"I'll pack, but still don't trust you right now," She replied.

She walked into the kitchen to sort out what she wanted to pack. Even thou she was upset with me, I could still see the excitement in her face. I went back to the truck and got the moving boxes. After setting them down in the living room, I started loading the truck with the hand truck. Once the significant items were loaded and secured, I started loading the boxes on the truck. I got the smallest truck they had because I didn't plan to take everything with me especially the bed. I don't know about most people, but I believe in the transferring of spirits. When you are starting a new life, you can't take everything with you. Somethings serve a greater purpose buried in the past. You can't even allow them to be in your rearview mirror because temptation is nothing to play with. After a few hours, we had everything in the truck.

"Well, that looks like everything Stacy."

"Are you sure about leaving all this stuff behind? Most of it still looks brand new."

I took one last look around before giving a response. "What's left behind will serve no purpose in our future. Now, let's go see the new place I found," I said while closing the front door for the last time.

We all jumped in, putting Gabriele in the middle. Her little face was just happy to be riding in a truck. "Daddy, Where we going?"

"Daddy is taking you and mommy somewhere better to live. It has a nice big playground with a bunch of kids your age."

"Mommy, did you hear that, I'm going to have new friends to play with."

"Yes sweetheart. Let's wait until we arrive before we get our hopes up. Daddy can tell some good stories."

I didn't say a word because my mood was in a great place right now. Stacy is always on edge. This house won't ease all her fears, but hopefully it's a start of better things to come. As we round the last corner, I watched their facial expressions. The house was two story brick with black shutters. It had a double garage, and the driveway was paved down to the road.

"Frank, don't tell me this is our new house!!! This thing is huge. How can we make the payments?"

"Let's get inside and unpack before we talk finances. Just enjoy the moment for once in your life."

At that point, she didn't speak another word. Of course I'm not going to tell her I used some of the drug money to get this place. I'm struggling with it myself. I can't take back how this money came into my life. At least some of it will serve a greater good. I didn't show up to town holy and sanctified. My sins are longer than I care to list. The blood of Jesus has washed them away and truly given us a chance to do better. If for no better reason than to give my daughter a life she would not have back home. I owe her at least that much. I backed the truck up close to the door as I could. Was not about to tear up the freshly cut grass. Stacy went straight to the front door. "Would you please come and open this door. I want to see my house."

"Your house now. Look who done a 360 from a few days ago. Can I put the break on first?" After getting the truck secured, I opened the front door so they could go inside. I forgot the paperwork in the front seat.

"Stacy, I forgot something in the truck I'll be right back."

I ran out and reached into passenger side window to get them. Just as I was about to go into the house, that same Chrysler 300 came cruising by. I walked back to the curb throwing

both hands up in the air. "What I'm right here!!"
I yelled out. Whoever it was sped off. The
windows were tinted too dark for me to see who
was in the car. Part of whatever I left back in
Detroit has followed me to Fall River Mills. This
one may be worse than James ever was. Lord,
please don't let me have to backslide. Whatever
it takes to keep my family safe, even if it's my
life. Let me pull it together, and try to enjoy the
moment at least. First thing in the morning, I'll
deal with this mess. Good thing the rest of the
money is in a bank safety deposit box across
town.

*******************

## Stacy

Look at all this house, this is sure a long way from the projects of Detroit. Where in the world did he get all this new furniture? Hope he didn't go back to selling on the streets. I ran around the house like a kid in the candy store. The first place to check out was the master bedroom. Soon as my feet walked in the room, I was blown away by the size of it. You could fit my old apartment in here. Let me see the bathroom, now this what I'm talking about. Double sinks, garden tub and a walk-in shower. Oh, he knows I'm putting it on him tonight, and then I'll find out where he got this stuff.

Let me go back downstairs before my child thinks her mother went crazy. When I reached the top of the steps, I stopped dead in my tracks. Just to watch my family playing on the floor of our first home was priceless. The way Gabriele is jumping around, I think I'll nickname her Gabby after that famous gymnast. By the time I reached the bottom of the stairs, I was in tears.

"Mommy, why are you crying? Did my daddy do something wrong?"

"Come here baby. No your daddy didn't do anything wrong. Mommy is just happy about this beautiful home he got us," I explained.

Gabby has seen me cry more than I care to mention. Not having her father around was hard on the both of us. I know he left me with the money, but I never touched a dime. Spending that kind of money in the hood draws too much-unwanted attention.

"So by the big smile on your face, you love the house."

"You did alright. It's a little small for my taste but I can work with it."

We gather together on the sofa and just enjoyed some family time. Life is good for once.

## Kelly

My whole body feels so weak this morning like I got hit by a car. I didn't even hear Rodney leave out for work. Let me see if I can make it to the bathroom. Ok legs, let's get you off this bed. So far so good. Now see if the rest will cooperate. That hurt more than usual but I'm up. Now to see if I can make it the rest of the way. My legs feel like a ton of bricks. Would you look at my hair, it's just a mess. This cough of mine is getting worse these days. Just as I was reaching for my toothbrush, I started coughing real bad.

When I thought it was calming down, one big one came out of nowhere. When I opened my eyes, there was blood all over the mirror and sink. It was also running down my nightgown. Lord, please don't let this be my time. I have so much more that I want to do. Least give me a chance to say goodbye to my husband. Still coughing up blood, I made it back to the bed. I reached over and hit my medical alert button. Rodney had it put in last month when I didn't answer the phone. "This is Life Alert. Mrs.

Campbell are you ok?" A male voice asked. "Please send help! I'm coughing up blood," Sounding frantic

"I dispatched an ambulance and called your husband," He replied.

The person on the other end was doing their best to keep me calm down, but I couldn't hold back my emotions. The tears started mixing with the blood on my clothes. I tried to stay upright but my body was too weak, and I fell over onto the bed. The more I coughed, the more blood would come out. Please Lord, let the ambulance hurry up and get here. Being I was sleep when Rodney left, I have no idea where he is this morning. Just as I was about to blackout, I heard the ambulance pulling up outside. Thank you Lord, for getting them here safely. They know where the spare keys are so the front door won't have to be damaged. I hear them coming up the stairs now.

"Lord please don't take me without letting me look into my husband's eyes one more time."

"It's ok Mrs. Campbell, we got you," said one of the paramedics.

"Thank you for getting here so fast, and please excuse all the blood," I replied.

They loaded me on the stretcher right before I blacked out.

************

# Rodney

I was on my way to my next showing when my cell phone wrong.

"Hello, this is Rodney. Great day to buy a home," I answered.

"Mr. Campbell, this is Life Alert. Your wife is being rushed to the hospital with an unknown medical emergency," Said the caller.

"Oh my Lord, I knew I shouldn't have left her home alone today. If something happens to her, I don't know what I will do," Sounding scared.

"Mr. Campbell, are you going to be ok to drive to the hospital?"

"Yes, I'll be okay. Thank you for calling," I replied.

I turned around in the middle of the road and headed to the hospital. When I looked at the dashboard, I was going over 100 MPH. Getting a ticket was the least of my concerns. I made it to the hospital the same time an ambulance was turning in. I didn't know if she was on that one so I parked in the ER parking lot. I rushed to the check-in desk. "My wife is being brought in for a medical emergency."

"What is her name sir?" The lady asked.

"Her name is Kelly Campbell. Please hurry, I need to know what's going on!"

"She is being seen by the doctors now. I will have a nurse bring you back."

"Thank you and I'm sorry for yelling."

"I understand sir. Please stand over by that door, they should be right out."

While I was waiting, I pulled out my cell phone to call her parents to let them know she was here. Just when I was about to call Kerry, the nurse called my name.

"Yes, I'm Mr. Campbell. How is my wife doing?"

"I'll let the doctor talk to you more private in the back," she said.

She led me to a large room where Kelly was lying in bed. She looked so weak and tired. They had her hooked up to all kinds of machines that were either humming or beeping. I knew this was not just one of her frequent episodes. My first emotion was to cry, but I knew I had to show strength right now. I walked over to hold her hand.

"Honey, I'm so sorry for being sick," She said.

"Don't talk like that. We are in this together. I love you with all my soul and would gladly trade places with you in a heartbeat. When I said I do, it was for times like these."

"That's why I'm so glad God blessed me with a good man. I love you Rodney Campbell, and I'm so happy you were the one on the bridge that day."

Just as we both were about to start crying, the doctor came into the room.

"Knock, knock, I'm Doctor Weaver," He said.

"Hello Doctor Weaver, I'm Rodney, Kelly's husband. Can you please tell me what is going on with my wife?"

"It looks like you wife is having a bad reaction to the increased chemo treatments. We are moving her to a room upstairs," He explained.

I have so many more questions to ask, but I'll wait to speak with her doctor.

**\*\*\*\*\*\*\*\*\*\*\*\*\*\***

## Kerry

"Get out of my way! Where is my cousin Kelly Campbell?" I shouted.

"Miss, I need you to lower your voice in the hospital, please. Now if you give me your family member's name, I can look her up in the system," Replied the nurse.

"Are you deaf and dumb? I gave you her name when I walked in here. Get me somebody that can help me now!!" Just when she was about to say something, I noticed a security guard walking over to me. I know he doesn't think he is going to tell me what to do.

"Miss, you are going to have to calm down or leave the hospital. We can't help you acting like this."

"Kerry Walker, if you don't settle yourself down." I know that voice.

When I turned around, I saw my Aunt and Uncle coming through the sliding glass doors. I haven't seen them both in years. That's because every time I see my Uncle, I see my uncle's face who raped me. Well also because my Aunt and I don't see eye to eye on things about my life.

"Officer, she won't be any more trouble. Now if someone can please tell us what room my daughter is in, please. Her name is Kelly Campbell."

"She has been moved to a private room upstairs. It's room 4234," Replied the nurse.

"Thank you for your help nurse. Kerry if you can settle down, you can come along."

We didn't say a word to each other which was fine with me. We made our way to the elevator and found her floor. I stayed in the back while my Uncle led the way to her room. Once in the room, I broke down in tears seeing Kelly hooked up to all the machines. I pushed passed everyone to be closer to her. I took her hand so she knew I was there.

"Hello, Mr. and Mrs. Franklin, thanks for coming so fast. I'm waiting for her doctor to get here to tell me what is going on," Said Rodney.

"Rodney, what happen this time? How is her chemo treatments going?" Asked my aunt.

"The doctor in the ER said, he believes it may be a reaction to the treatments. We just have to pray for the best now."

I know he just didn't ask them to pray. My Uncle hardly went to church, and my Aunt only goes when it suits her needs. Maybe if they went to church more, things would have turned out different. My aunt looked like she was about to say something when the Doctor walked into the room.

"Sorry for keeping you, but I wanted to read her results first. Let me just check her vital signs before we get started," He said. We all moved back so he could do what he needed. Kelly was still sleeping due to the medication she was given. I need to talk to her, but I know she needs to rest.

"Well, she seems to be sleeping well now. I know you all have many questions so I won't beat around the bush. Kelly's lung cancer is spreading faster than the chemo can keep up. At this point, there is nothing more that modern medicine can do for her. All we can do now is keep her as comfortable as possible. Hopefully, we can make arrangements to have her moved to hospice care tomorrow afternoon. I know this may not be what you wanted to hear, but we have come to that time."

**\*\*\*\*\*\*\*\*\*\*\*\*\*\*\***

## Rodney

His words went right through my heart like a dull butter knife. Even though I knew this might be coming, I still gave it all to God. The doctors tell us one thing, but we as believers know who has the last word. I could see they all were waiting for me to say something. Kelly didn't tell any of them her cancer had spread. Well, I'm not going to throw my wife under the bus.

"First, let me tell everyone that the decision not to tell you about the cancer spreading was both of ours. We thought she would get better with the increase in chemo treatments."

"How could you both keep something like this from us? You know what she means to me. As her mother, I should have been kept up to date on her health."

"Rodney, I been over to your house more times than I remember. I didn't see any signs of her health getting worse because she was doing so good with the meds," Kerry shouted.

"Kerry, your cousin was good at hiding how she felt until you were gone. She sometimes would spend hours in the bathroom throwing up due to the chemo. Now you can sit here blaming me for what is happening, but that's not going to take away the fact my wife is lying here dying."

"Rodney, no one is throwing shade son. We just wish you would have come to us about our daughter. As her father, I could have been here more to support you both. Now what are your plans going forward?"

"Plans, I'm still trying to adjust to this news. How can you prepare for losing your soul mate? I need time to think of what to do next. It's all too much right now."

I begin to pace back and forth crying, and really unsure of what to do about this.

*******************

## Kelly

I came around lying in a hospital room. It took a minute for my eyes to adjust to the lights, but I could make out my family in the room. What are my parents doing here with Kerry? It must be worse than the last time. I hate seeing my husband cry over me, but I know it's out of love. I just hope they haven't been beating him up too much over not telling them anything.

"Honey, please don't cry. Come here and hold my hand," I said loud as I could.

Everyone stopped what they were doing and came over to my bed. I know this is killing my father on the inside and my mother worse.

"Kelly, how do you feel sweetheart? Look at me asking stupid questions."

"It's ok baby; I know you're scared right now. Even though we talked about it many times, I'm still not ready for what is coming. I just need for you to be strong for the both of us right now."

"Kelly, is there anything we can do for you, sweetheart?" My father asked.

"I'm just glad you both are here with us. Please don't give Rodney a hard time for not telling you anything. It was me that asked him not to tell anyone. Everyone worrying was not going to make me better, and you were already in prayer over my condition. Let's just focus on where we are now, please. What did the doctor say and please don't lie to me?"

"Honey, the doctor said you have gotten worse. The cancer is spreading, and the chemo is doing nothing to stop it. They want to move you to hospice to keep you comfortable as possible," He said while breaking down again.

I could hear the pain in his voice. Is he saying what I think, and is this my last days living? If it is, Lord I'm ready to be welcome into your arms because this body is so tired.

*********************

# Frank

Last night was great spending time with my family. I hate going to work, but the bills are going to be bigger now with my new responsibilities. Even though that might be the case, I wouldn't have it any other way. Little Gabby is like a breath of fresh air. Thank you Lord, for allowing me to come into her life while she is still a child. Just thinking of her growing up without a father in her life like I did is heartbreaking.

After getting my usual coffee and breakfast biscuit, I headed to the yard. I'm starting to like being a business owner, but I will not let it go to my head. I don't see Jake this morning which is not normal; he usually beats me here. After parking, I went to the front office to go over the bills for this month. Two hours later, I heard Jake pulling up outside.

"Good Morning partner, how is everything going?"

"I was about to blow up your cell phone looking for you. It's the first time I ever saw you come to work late. Is everything ok?"

"I never had a business partner that I could take time away from work. It sure felt good to sleep in late this morning. Now that you're here, maybe I can take a vacation somewhere other than the lake. I see you been going over the bills, how are they looking?"

"Everything is paid up to date except these right here. I wasn't sure what accounts they went with so I left them for you."

I handed him everything I had not paid. We both talked for a while before getting to work. Mondays are mostly slow, but today was more like a Saturday. Seem like every shade tree mechanic was here today. We may need to look into hiring another person if this keeps up. I was glad when 5:00 came because my body was running out of fuel. I took care of the last few customers before locking up. Jake went home about an hour ago; he loves this partner thing. I headed back to the family which is the best part of my day now. Halfway home I get this weird feeling like when I was selling on the block. I pushed the pedal to the floor not caring about stop lights or police. I had to be doing over 120 MHP through town; I made it to my driveway without getting stopped. I jumped out running to the front door. I looked through the living room window, but I didn't see any movement in the house. The way Gabby runs around nonstop, I knew something was wrong. I went back to my car, getting my heat from the glovebox.

I went around back to catch whoever was in the house off guard. I turned the door handle slowly keeping the gun facing down in case Gabby was in the area. I still didn't hear any signs of anyone in the house; every room look like a storm came through. Who could have done this? Oh my God if anything happens to them I would die. I pulled out my cell phone to call Stacy; It's ringing that's good.

"Hello Sweetheart, are you both ok?" I asked sounding worried.

"Hello, Frank!" A male voice answered.

"Who is this and where is my family?" I demanded

"Shut up Frank, I'll give the orders around here. I'm only going to ask you one time, and if I have to ask a second time, you won't like what comes next," He said.

It was Delgado the drug connect from Detroit. How in the world did he find us? The thought of him having my family sent a rage through my body. Now I know where I saw that Chrysler 300 from. It was parked on the curb the day we met with them. I told that fool James not to cross these people. Why are they holding me responsible for the money he owes? That answers the question I had about the amount of money I found stuffed within the sofa that he put there. It was over ten thousand dollars, and I used every dime on his home going service.

"I need to know my family is safe before I agree to anything," I demanded again.

"There you go again, thinking you are in charge. Your little family is safe just as long as I get my money. Did you clowns think you could steal from me without consequences? Now I want my fifty thousand dollars, and I want you to bring it to me personally. Frank, we both know what will happen if you bring the cops into this."

Fifty thousand dollars? Then where is the other forty thousand. Knowing the old James, he spent it on women and parties. I can't believe this mess right now.

"How did you find me here?" I said.

"You can thank your lovely lady friend here for that. My people were tailing her when we couldn't find you. I knew it was just a matter of time before she got lovesick and came looking for her man. You have a gorgeous little child; I would hate to see anything happen to her."

"If you touch one hair on her head, I'll hunt you down and kill you!!! Now let me speak to Stacy!" I shouted.

"You can talk to her for one second and don't get stupid asking questions."

"Frank!! Help us, please. We don't want to die. I didn't hear them come into the house until it was too late," She screamed.

"Are you satisfied now? Let's get back to my money. I want you to bring it back to Detroit this weekend. I'll call you with the time and place tomorrow. About that last statement of yours, I won't have to touch a hair on her head because I'll be sending it to you in the mail. Now be a good boy and bring me my money!" He hung up before I could respond.

I started tossing things around in a fit of rage. The way this place looks, they were searching for the money James took. They must have been following me around town for a while. Buying this house must have him thinking I have the money. It burns me up when people assume you're doing something wrong when you try and better yourself or your living situation. I used my own darn money to get this house and now look at it. I didn't forget where the money came from in the first place but was I going to throw it in the trash. Anyone can second guess your life, but ask them if they are willing to trade places with you. My mind is telling me to go back and kill everyone involved in taking my family. My heart is telling me to give it all to the Lord. I placed my gun down on the kitchen counter just staring at it. I can see this gun, and I know its power from personal experience. I went upstairs to get my mother's Bible; once I found it I placed it down on the other side of the gun. I can see this book and read its words, but I never seen Jesus or the Lord in person. In my short personal experience with them, I truly have seen the mighty power of the word of God. I'm at a crossroads right now in who do I trust with my family's life.

Lord, what do you want me to do? You brought them back into my life just when I needed them the most. If I knew spending that money would have led to this, I would have never bought this house. Gabby is not even two years old, and I've already got her caught up in the game. I turned my life around and became a better person. Please help me to understand how this could happen under your watch. I know the word says not to question you which I'm trying my best not to do. I just want my family back safely. I could take this gun and kill them all, but taking a life is a sin that may cost me my salvation. I could take you at your word and place everything in your hands. What do I do?

**\*\*\*\*\*\*\*\*\*\*\*\*\***

## Stacy

"Calm down baby girl, your daddy is coming to get us," I said trying to reassure her. I had just placed her down for a nap when they rushed into the house. I ran downstairs to keep them from getting to her, but I was thrown down to the floor by two guys. I watched another one run up and returned carrying Gabby. One was stepping on my back so I couldn't get up. Once they tied us up, they started tearing the house apart which at the time I didn't know what they were looking for.

After about thirty minutes, one of them came over to the sofa where they had placed us. He was in my face, yelling for me to tell him where the money was. Every time I said I didn't know, he would slap me across the face causing Gabby to cry louder which made him upset. Not knowing what he would do to her, I begged her to stop crying. I hated being powerless to help her, but he knew looking into my eyes that I would give my life for her. I'm not sure where we are, but from his conversation with Frank, I knew we are back in Detroit. Wait, I can hear someone coming. "Whatever you do sweetie, don't cry," I told Gabby.

"Here is some food to eat. I don't need you two dying on me," He said tossing a couple of sandwiches at me. "Why are you doing this? My child and I have done nothing to you," I said.

"From the looks of you and all the tattoos, I'm thinking you know how the games goes. Let's not insult each other's intelligence, you might live longer. Don't worry, no one here is going to touch you or your daughter sexually. You can get that look off your face."

"How long do you plan on keeping us locked in this room?"

"Now that's going to be up to Frank won't it? All he has to do is bring me the money."

He said slamming the door on his way out. I just hope Frank doesn't do anything stupid.

## Mother Mary

"I hear you Lord, give me a minute to get these old bones moving," I replied. Awaken from my sleep by troubling dreams. I didn't know what was going on, but I knew to be obedient to the Holy Spirit. It was time to get into my prayer closet, but first I went to get a glass of water from the kitchen because something told me I was going to be in there a while.

"I'm here Lord; please allow the Holy Spirit to show me what to pray for," I said as I went into prayer.

As I was praying, the Lord laid Deacon Mosley and his family, Kerry and Pastor, Sister Kelly and Brother Rodney on my heart.

"Father, in the mighty name of Jesus, I plead the blood over each and every one of their lives. Father, I stand in intercession first for Deacon Mosely and his family. I fear the worst storm that your man will face has come to pass. His family is in danger Father, and he will do anything to save them. I feel his faith is going to be tested like never before Father. He is a young convert who based on his first sermon knows how to face battles on the street, but Father he has no idea how to fight battles of spiritual warfare. His love for you is strong, but his anger is allowing the devil to pull him away from you.

Father, I pray that you will send the Holy Spirit his way to reassure him of your love and remind him that vengeance is yours. Where ever his family is Lord, keep them self until you can rescue them. Dispatch your angles to comfort them Father, and I pray that you touch the hearts of whoever has placed them in danger. Father, I only met his lady friend and his child once, so I don't know where their faith stands. Something is telling me it's not where it should be, but their hearts are open to receive you. Father this is the perfect situation for you to show yourself strong. Wrap them in your love and show yourself mighty in their lives so when this is over they will have no doubt that you are the Alpha and the Omega."

"Father, I now come to you in intercession for Pastor Walker and First Lady Walker. Lord, I'm way too old to beat around the bush so let's get right to it. You already know this marriage is a hot mess from head to toe. They both have been putting on this fake facade for years that even these old eyes could see right through. Because you called him, Father we as the church dare not second guess that. Thank goodness he is a mighty man of God.

His love for that woman is as strong as his love for you. I can see his heartbreaking sometimes when they are together. Devil you will not destroy this marriage. Jesus said in the book of Mark, chapter 10 verses 8 -10, **"And they twain shall be one flesh: so then they are no more twain, but one flesh. What therefore God hath joined together, let not man put asunder."**

So you see that not even you have the power to tear them apart. So I plead the blood of Jesus Christ over their marriage. Father, I pray that you will touch Kerry's heart and allow her to face her worst fears and come back to you. Whatever hurt she has been carrying around that she releases it into your hands."

"Last but not lease Father. I come to you in intercession for Brother Rodney and Sister Kelly. Pastor Walker has already told us to keep them in prayer. I come to you more for Brother Rodney Father. If it's your well to call Sister Kelly home, then guard his heart. He will need you more than ever. Father his whole world will be crashing down around him, but it's not the end of his life. Father show him the reason for going on and that her love for him would want the same. Plant the people in place that when the time comes they will be there. I know she has been suffering in her body and it's only getting worse. Comfort her father and allow her to have peace."

"It says in your word in the book of Lamentations 3:31-33, ***"For no one is cast off by the Lord forever. Though he brings grief, he will show compassion, so great is his unfailing love. For he does not willingly***

**bring affliction or grief to anyone."** Father, you also teach us in the book of Ecclesiastes 3:1-4, **"To everything there is a season, a time to every purpose under the heaven: a time to be born, a time to die, a time to plant, and a time to pluck up that which is planted; A time to kill, and a time to build up; A time to weep, and a time to laugh, a time to mourn and a time to dance."**

Father, I hope that I have touched on every need that needs to be met. I know your will in each of these matters will be done. My heart just pours out for that little girl in all this; she is way too young to endure such pain. I just wish I knew more about what is going on, but then I wouldn't be called a prayer warrior now would I. We are called into battle when it becomes spiritual. For it says in the book of Ephesians 6:12, **"For we wrestle not against flesh and blood, but against the rulers of the darkness of this world, against spiritual wickedness in high places."**

Lord, I hope my service to your people has been a righteous one and not one of selfishness. I don't know how many more years of life I have left upon this earth to do your work, but whatever time I have it will be for your glory.

This prayer closet has seen many battles some have been all out war. If these old walls could talk, they would have some stories to tell starting with my own battles. Thank you Lord, for allowing me to become a seasoned believer. Now with that being said, you are the beginning and the end, you never sleep or slumber and a thousand years are but a day to you. That's why I love you, Lord. As for me, these old bones can't stay up past the nightly news. I will end this prayer session like as I always do in the mighty name of Jesus Christ. Amen and Amen." I placed my prayer bible down on my rocking chair and went to bed for the night. It's all in the hands of the Lord now.

# Frank

As I was trying to put the living room back together, I started getting this feeling like someone had been praying for me. My mind was at peace and the book of Isaiah 41:10 came into my spirit. I went and picked up my mother's Bible and found the scripture. It says, **"So do not fear, for I am with you; do not be dismayed, for I am your God. I will strengthen you and help you; I will uphold you with my righteous right hand."**

It I had to guess who it was that was praying for me, I would say it was Mother Mary. Don't know how she can tell when something is wrong, but I'm blessed to have her in my corner. I was planning to take things into my hands and load up the truck with heat. Instead, I'm going to believe in the Lord just like he believed in me. My faith may not be where Mother Mary's is but in the book of Matthew chapter 17 verse 20 it reads, **"And Jesus said unto them, because of your unbelief: for verily I say unto you, if ye have faith as a grain of a mustard seed, ye**

**shall say unto this mountain, remove hence to yonder place; and it shall remove; and nothing shall be impossible unto you."**

Jesus was talking to his disciples and was getting on them when then asked why they couldn't rebuke the devil out of a possessed child. Even though they were with him in the flesh, when it came time to exercise their faith; fear of what they couldn't see took control. I was about to do the same thing concerning my faith. I pulled my cell phone from my pocket, took a few deep breaths then dialed Officer Jones, who was now a detective.

"Detective Jones, how can I help you please?" He answered.

"Detective Jones, this is Deacon Mosely. Do you have time to talk with me?"

"Hey Frank, what's on your mind?" He replied.

I was starting to get second thoughts when I realized bringing the police into this may get my family killed. I trusted him with James, and I'm still alive. Here goes nothing. "Detective Jones, I'm going to come straight to the reason for this call because I don't have a lot of time. My family is in danger and being held by a drug cartel back in Detroit."

"Frank, remember when I asked you that day at the store if anything was going on in my town I needed to know and is this part of that conversation?" He said sounding upset.

"Yes, and I'm sorry for not being upfront before. That Chrysler 300 I mention had been following me around town for I don't know how long. It showed up shortly after my fiancée did," I explained.

"What is the connection between you and this car?" He asked.

"They were my drug connect, and now they want the money James took from them. If I don't bring it in person on Saturday, then my family is dead. He even threaten to send my little girl's head to me in a box."

"Wow, is all I can say. When you get caught up in something, it's made for television drama." He said laughing.

"Look, I don't have time to be the source of your humor. If you're not going to help me, then I'll handle things myself," I said while hanging up on him.

I didn't expect him to take it so lightly which got me turned up fast. "Lord, I tried to do the right thing, but you see how that turned out." I went back to packing what I needed to get my family back. I made a few phone calls to people back in Detroit I know I can still trust to be down with me. When I came downstairs, my eyes went straight over to where I had placed my mother's Bible.

"I'm sorry mother, but I need to get my family back. I thought you said I could hide in the Lord. Is this what you call hiding?" I said before getting ready to go out the door. Just when I was closing the front door, her Bible fell off the table. I placed my bags down and went over to pick it up. It turned to the book of

Proverbs chapter 29, and my finger was resting on verse 11 which reads, **'A fool gives full vent to his anger, but a wise man keeps himself under control.'**

After reading that, I knew my mother's spirit was still with me. I flopped down on the sofa and started weeping. The only thing I could think of was the time wasted while Stacy and Gabby are going through God knows what. "Lord, send me some help, please!!" I shouted out loud. Just when I was about to throw the lamp against the wall, there was a knock at the front door. Who could that be because no one knew where I moved to yet. I walked over to the front door being careful just in case Deangelo sent his people to take me out.

"Who is it?" I yelled through the door.

"Frank open the door, it's me, Detective Jones," He replied.

I opened the door allowing him to enter. "Frank, you were not kidding, look at this place. You have to accept my apology, but I was not taking your situation lightly. I was merely trying to ease the tension in your voice; you hung up without hearing me out. Now if you are ready to listen, I believe I can help get your family back safely," He explained.

"Yes and forgive me as well. When it comes to your family, you know how it is. What do you have in mind?" I asked.

"Well, I made a few phone calls to some friends of mine in the FBI, and they are willing to help on the case. When I told them it was the drug cartel, they were all in. I need to know what their demands are so we can devise a plan to get your family out safely," He explained.

"He wants me to bring fifty thousand dollars to him, and he is going to call me with the place and time," I said keeping it straight to the point.

"What is this guy's name, Frank?" He asked.

"I just know him as Deangelo, wish I could tell you more."

"That maybe good enough for my friends at the FBI; they have a much larger database than we do here," He explained.

"All this waiting is killing me; I'm doing my best to keep my emotions from getting the best of me."

"Don't lose control now Frank. We will get your family back I promise. Just give us time to do what we do best. You say that God is your source right?"

"Yes, he is my source and my peace," I answered.

"That's what I wanted to hear. Now don't lose hold to that," He replied.

He finished telling me everything that he was going to do, and I filled in whatever information I could add to his plan. After about an hour, he left to go back to the police station to make some phone calls. I went back to trying to put my house back together which will help keep my mind off seeking revenge. Just makes me mad to see Gabby's toys are crushed all over the floor. I know I'm stepping into the father role for the first time, but my love for her is without measure. I just wish this phone would ring already I'm ready to get this over.

**\*\*\*\*\*\*\***

# Kelly

"Thank you nurse. Can you please have no one disturb me for about thirty minutes, please," I asked.

"Yes. I will post a note on your door for everyone to come to the nurse's station before coming into your room," She said.

I waited until she left out before getting out of bed. I walked over taking my Bible from my belongings. I was moved here from the hospital yesterday, and I haven't had time to unpack. No matter how much you do and have in life, you can never be prepared for this. I took my Bible and returned to my bed. Walking around has got me feeling light headed.

"Lord, this is Kelly and of course, you already know this," I laughed. "I wanted to spend some alone time with you. I don't blame you for what is happing to my body. I'm holding fast to 2 Corinthians 5:8 which says, **"We are confident, I and willing rather to be absent from the body, and to be present with the**

***Lord.*"** I love you more for the life you allowed me to live. I wanted to jump off that bridge that day, but you had other plans for my life. If I had any regrets, it would be not being able to give Rodney a child. He never shows it, and that's why I love him so much. If I could go back and change anything in my life, it would be that night Kerry got assaulted by Uncle Ron.

I would have screamed out loud and maybe she wouldn't have to bear this hurt as I do. Death will end my inner stuffing, but it won't help heal the blame I placed on myself. I need to get it right with her before I close my eyes to this world forever. Well thank you, Father, for spending time with me. It's always good to know what a great listener you are."

I placed my Bible on the table and got back in bed because I was feeling weak. I pushed the call button for my nurse.

"Yes Mrs. Campbell, is everything alright?" she asked

"I'm feeling drained, can you check my vitals, please?" I said sounding worried. While she was checking them, I could hear Kerry coming down the hallway. That cousin of mine has no filter.

"I don't want to have to buzz that door that long again or I will have someone's job do you understand!!" She yelled at the nursing staff.

"Girl, get in here and leave those people alone. What are you doing here this early? I thought you said you were coming this afternoon."

"I just couldn't sit around at home when I could be here with you. Look, I know we both trust the Lord, but I don't know when he's going to call you home. I love you so much Kelly, and it's hard seeing my life without you in it," She said before she broke out crying.

"See, now you got me tearing up. Come and sit beside me on the bed, I want to talk to you," I said while reaching for the tissue box.

"What's on your mind cousin? Let me know if sitting here starts hurting you?" She said as she sat down.

"Hand me that glass of water please," I replied.

I took a few sips before handing it back to her. I needed to gather my thoughts before I started this next conversation because I knew it would be very emotional for the both of us. It was now time to clear my conscience of any past sins.

"Kerry, I need to confess something to you, and before you interrupt, let me finish, please. It is vital to my salvation."

"Kelly, whatever it is, can't it wait until you are feeling better?"

"We both know that this is only going to end one way so let me make peace with you alright," I pleaded.

"Alright, I can see in your eyes that this means a lot," She replied.

"Kerry, about that night at the house when we were little."

"Kelly, please don't bring up that evening at a time like this," She shouted.

"Kerry, come back over here and sit down. I need to get this out, and you are going to listen."

"Find, but don't expect me to keep my emotions uncontrolled."

"Now, about that night at the house when you stayed over. I was not sleeping when Uncle Ron took you. I felt you trying to pull on the sheets so he couldn't remove you from the bed. I heard you trying to kick and scream for him to let you go. When I heard the room door close, I jumped up out of the bed and ran over to the door. I opened it enough to see him taking you down to the basement. I knew that was where he was taking you because he would take me to the same place. I wanted to scream, but nothing would come out. I was so frightened and thought he would come back for me. I jumped back into bed and balled up near the wall. I broke out crying just thinking of what he was doing to you. When I heard him bringing you back, I jumped back under the cover and pretended to be sleep.

I heard him telling you not to say anything, or he would kill your family. Can you find it in your heart to forgive me for allowing that to happen to you? I watched over the years how that night has badly impacted your life. Running from man to man. I know you love your husband, but you have to first love yourself. I love you enough to come clean, but I hate it has to come on my death bed. I'm asking you in the name of Jesus to get your life in order before it's too late. Remember that God loves the sinner not the sin and all you have to do is ask for forgiveness."

Before I could continue, she gets up and goes over to the window. "Kelly, your words are hurtful and a blessing at the same time. I waited for years to hear those words come from your lips. About that night at your house. I knew you were not sleeping. You have never been good at faking anything. I don't blame you for what happen, and I already forgiven you years ago.

As far as my sleeping around with different men, I should have stopped years ago. I don't know when, but at some point, I started to enjoy what I was doing. It was like I was the one in control of men and not them over me. Uncle Ron really did a number on my head and closed off my heart to love. It wasn't until I met my husband that I opened it back up. He showed me the love I never thought I could have. When he introduced me to God, who fixed my broken spirit. I can say I wasn't driven by lust, but it was the power that fueled my passion. I hated when any man was lying on top of me, but I loved the power I had over their lives. It's only now, seeing you like this that I realize I become the very monster I hated."

"Kerry, you still have time to get your soul right. You can walk away from that life and become the woman of God I know you are. Come pray the sinner's prayer with me while I still have breath in my body," I pleaded.

"Wait, please let me run out to the car and get something. I have something I want you to see and read before we do this. I'll be right back," She said while running out the door.

I laid back down and rested my eyes. Talking with Kerry is always draining on me.

## Rodney

I was coming down the hallway when I saw Kerry heading in my direction. I knew something happen because of the tears in her eyes.

"Kerry, is everything alright with Kelly?

"Yes. Everything is just wonderful, I'm just running out to my car to get something. It's great to see you," She said without breaking a stride.

I stopped by the nurse's station to get an update on Kelly's condition. They told me she is getting weaker by the hour, and she refused to let them increase her morphine drip. I thanked them before heading to her room. When I walked in, her eyes were closed as if she was at peace. I walked over taking her hand and fearing the worse.

"Honey, when did you come in? I must have dozed off," She said.

"Oh thank you. I thought you had left me. I just walked in just now," I said while blowing a breath of relief.

"I been fighting to hold on till you came back. Sweetheart, I'm so tired and my body can't endure much more. I made peace with the people in my life. Please tell my parents how much I love them, and please don't take too much time grieving over my death. They wanted to come over, but I told them to wait until you called. I didn't want them watching me pass away. I need their last memory of me to be a happy one and not this.

I hope they will understand after everything has settled back down. Now that my eyes have seen yours, I'm ready to leave this world. I don't want you to spend much time grieving either. Keep me in your heart but move on with your life. Promise me that because I know you keep your word. I will always love you, and my heart will always be yours. I'll be in heaven praising the Lord with the rest of the saints. Now give me one last kiss goodbye."

"I promise my love, even if I don't agree. You will always live in my heart, and I will always love you. My heart wants to tell you not to leave, but my faith knows you will be in a better place. I know I can never replace the love we share and would never try. If the Lord sees fit to have that door open again, I will try not to slam it back close. For now, I will spend my time grieving as I should be allowed."

Just as I was done talking, this beautiful smile came over her face and she slipped away into paradise. I pulled up a chair and held her hands to my face. I begin to sing in a low voice.

"I love you, Lord, I love you, Lord, I love you Lord because you been so good to me." She used to sing it to herself whenever she was doing housework.

"Ok, Kelly I found it. Let me read it to you," Kerry said when she walked into the room.

"Kerry, Kelly is with the Lord now," I told her as she came closer to the bed.

"NO! NO! No!!!" She cried out. I stood up to comfort her because I know how her emotions can get the best of her. Placing my arms around her to let her know we will get through this, she began to beat on my back with her fist which I understood.

"Rodney, I just went to the car. Couldn't the Lord wait until I got back? I wanted her to see this picture of us before I went off to college. On the back, it read, "We will always be together in spirit." Why couldn't he let her see this before he took her from me?"

"We never know what the Lord plans are for our lives, but we can rejoice in the time he gives us with each other," I said trying to give both of us some peace. I then called Kelly's parents and began making plans for her home going service. I contacted Pastor Walker being he is our pastor and she would want him to give the eulogy.

# Frank

All this waiting around for the phone to ring is starting to get the best of me. My mind is slipping back towards going up there solo and getting my family back. Let me stop what I'm doing and go over to the church. I grabbed my car keys off the fireplace and headed out the door. I got halfway down the street before realizing I forgot my bible. I went to the next block and turned around going back to the house.

After getting inside, I found my Bible. Then I placed it back down to pick up my mother's bible. Hers has brought me so much peace since I had it in my possession. I was about to leave when I noticed Gabby's favorite toy near the sofa. It was the car I give her when she first got here. I picked it up placing it into my front pocket while holding back the tears. After getting back to the car and putting the Bible on the dashboard, I headed to the church. When I pulled into the parking lot, there was a not a car in sight which was unusual for this time of day. Being a Deacon I had the keys so I was able to get in with no problem.

I checked around and didn't find a soul in the building. I wondered where everyone could be. I made my way into the sanctuary to pray. I could have prayed at home just the same, but this is where my life took a turn for the better, and right now I needed that spiritual connection. I went down to my knees and begin to pray.

"Lord, it's me again, Frank Mosley. I know you are busy and have a lot going on with the terrible things happing around the word. I know you are very well aware of my current situation, and working to intervene. I'm here because my emotions are getting the best of me. I don't want to step out of your will and place them in more danger. I need your guides as which direction to take. The police are doing their best and I know they are human which causes great concern. I been on the other side of the law so I know how things can go wrong quickly. If there is anyway possible to get them back to me safely, I know you will find away."

I continue to pray pouring everything I had up to the Lord. I was on my knees for hours praying for a miracle to happen. I was running on empty and was about to get when I heard a little voice call out to me.

"Daddy, daddy, daddy, you weren't at home when we came back!" She said.

I went to turn around to get up and see who it was, but she had run straight into my arms pushing me back down to the floor.

"Wait, let me look at you. I can't believe you are really here," I said checking her for any injuries. "How in the world is this possible right now?" I said looking back toward the direction she came from. I had been in the sanctuary so long that my eyes had to adjust to the light coming through the doors. I saw three figures standing in the doorway. I picked up Gabby and started walking toward them. I was tired but I was not about let her out of my arms. I could see Stacy was in tears and looked like she been through hell. I couldn't make out the other two but one of them looked like Detective Jones.

When I got closer to them, Stacy came running down to us. "Frank, oh my God, you don't know how happy I am to see your face," She said

"Stacy, how can this be happing right now? How in the world did you both get away?" I asked

She wouldn't respond but just kept kissing my face all over. Even with her all over me, I wouldn't loosen my hold on Gabby. My head is spinning so badly and I need an answer to this reunion. I know the drug cartel just didn't let them walk away without a price. While she was hugging my neck, I noticed one of the shadowy figures making their way down to us. It was Detective Jones.

"Well Frank, your family is home safe and they are unharmed," He said.

"Yes they are but who made this happen? I didn't receive a phone call and I still have the money," I replied.

"Why don't you ask your wife to be for the answer to that question? I think you're going to be surprised by the response," He said while taking a seat across from where we were standing.

"Stacy, what is he talking about?" I asked.

"Frank, come sit down and I'll tell you everything," She replied.

We went and sat down two rows up from where Detective Jones was sitting. I placed Gabby in my lap. Even though we are in church, my fear of losing her again had me paranoid.

"Ok, please tell me how you got away?"

"It was your daughter who saved our lives," She started the conversation with a bang.

"How? What do you mean this little girl saved your lives?"

"Every time they would come into the room, she would break out yelling, my daddy is a preacher and he telling God on you. She would then get on her knees and pray. She did this to the point that the guy who was keeping us wanted to know what she was talking about. He said that you were a lowlife drug dealer who pushed cocaine down his own people's veins. He called me a hood rat like he really knows what one is. I told him to pull up your YouTube video and see for himself. I watched it myself before coming to find you."

"What YouTube video are you talking about Stacy?" I said very confused.

"It's the one of you talking about Redemption and the Hoopty. He stood over us and said he was going to decide our fate after watching it. He then walked out and locked the door, and I told Gabby we needed to pray. She said not to worry because God had sent an angel to watch over us and he been here the whole time." She paused.

"Please go on," I asked her while I continued to hold on to Gabby.

"I looked all around the room trying to see this angel she was talking about, but I didn't see any. I admit I did feel a strong presence around us. It was about two hours later when the door opened back up, and another man told us to get our things and come with him. He brought us downstairs and asked us to have a seat at the kitchen table. There was two women in the kitchen cooking food. One of them walked over and set out plates in front of us while the other one came placing food on them.

I wasn't sure if it was safe for us to eat so I told Gabby not to touch it. That's when the man who took us came into the room and picked up a folk eating from both plates. He looked like he had been crying or something. He said that he watched the video two times and each time it brought him to tears. He told me this,"

"I been in this business for most of my life so I know bull when I come across it. When I first met Frank, I didn't like him as much, from looking into his eyes, I knew he would not double-cross me. He was in the game to make money which made a great business partnership. That's why I couldn't understand why he just up and disappeared, but after seeing this video, it answered all my questions. That

James was a real piece of work. I never did like him either. He was just a means to an end. I can see now that Frank is not the same man I first met. I'm a hard-nosed businessman, but I do have a heart for the family."

"So what does that mean for my daughter and me," I asked him.

"For you and your daughter, that means I'm returning you back to your home in one piece. That story of the Hoopty did something to my spirit. After you both get done eating my people will be driving you back."

"What about the money you kept demanding," I asked.

"Tell Frank, that money is an early wedding gift from me to the three of you. I saw the ring on your hand so I know a wedding is coming. Let him also know that he won't have to watch over his shoulder after today because I'm erasing his debt. Now I'll be leaving but you will be in good hands for your trip back. I apologized for any traumatizing done to your child but you already know what kind of people we are."

"He was about to leave out the room when Gabby ran over and took him by the hand. He bent down to see what she wanted. She looked him in the face and said, "Mister I forgive you and Jesus love you." She then ran back over to me. Your baby girl didn't even cry. They brought us back and dropped us off in front of the police station. When we went inside, I asked for the policeman sitting there because I heard you mention his name. We went to the house but you were not home. Gabby said we would find you here talking to God."

"I'm just so glad to have you both back in my life, but who is that other man standing in the doorway?" I asked

"What man Frank? It was just the three of us who came here," She replied.

I turned to point out the person, but when I looked in that direction, he was gone. I placed Gabby down next to Stacy and ran into the lobby. I didn't see anyone so I ran to the parking lot. I looked far as I could see but still didn't find anyone. I walked back into the lobby to find everyone standing there.

"Frank, what's wrong with you? You are scaring Gabby," She said.

"Mommy, Daddy is not scaring me. He's just looking for the Angel that was with us in the car," Gabby said.

"What Angel sweetheart? There was no one else in the car but us three."

"Mommy, I told you it was the same one that was with us. He stayed with us until we were safe with Daddy. I told him goodbye before he left. Can we go home now, I'm tired?"

"Mommy is tired too sweetheart and ready to go home more than you know."

I looked over at my family standing there safe and sound with just a few minor scrapes. I then begin to run around shouting at the top of my lungs giving God all the glory. When I got to the third go-round, both Stacy and Gabby had joined me. We did a few more laps before coming to a stop in front of Detective Jones.

"I'm happy for you both to have your family back together. I need to be getting back to the station, but I will need to come to the house next week to complete my report on this case."

"Yes, that will be good. I want to thank you for everything you did for us."

"Oh no, I can't take any credit for this one. This was all the man upstairs doing, and without him, it may have turned out very badly. This experience has showed me that I need to come back to church like I used too. Deacon Mosely, you coming to this town has changed more lives for the better then you know. Now take your family home and get some rest. After hearing her story, I feel confident this chapter of your life is closed forever."

## Pastor Walker

Yes. Thank you for your help. I'll have one of the Deacons come by in the morning to pick everything up," I said as I hung up the phone.

Good. That is taken care of now let me give Deacon Mosely a call to let him know what is going on. Even though I knew this was coming, as a Pastor death is still hard to deal with. It's ringing

"Hello Pastor, now is not a good time for me."

"Is everything alright with you and the family? You sound a bit shaken up."

"Pastor, if I tell you everything that's been going on, you would not believe it. We can talk about that later if you don't mind, but if you are calling then I know it's important."

"I don't know if you heard, but First Lady Walker's cousin passed today. I have been calling around to start making plans for her home going service. I would like you to be part of this if you don't mind."

"Pastor, I'm truly sorry to hear that, and please give my condolences to First Lady. Whatever it is that you need, I'll be happy to take care of it."

"Right now, I just need you to make sure you have a well-pressed suit and bring your lovely family if you don't mind. I haven't had time to spend with them much. We will have the service at the church of course, and it will be tomorrow at 3:00 pm."

"Yes sir, I will, and my family would love to be there as well. Goodbye, Pastor."

After hanging up with him, I headed back to the house to check on Kerry. When I pulled up into the driveway, I noticed she had parked sideways. This told me that she was really upset by Kelly's passing. After pulling her car into the garage, I went in through the garage door. I didn't see her downstairs so I went up to the bedroom.

"Honey, are you doing ok?" I asked.

I knew that's a loaded question to ask someone when they are going through, but it still has to be done.

"Yes I'm fine. I just wanted to be alone for a while. Thank you for helping with the arrangements for Kelly."

"Everything is done now we just have to get through the next few days. I know this is not what you wanted to be doing again."

"You are correct about that, but this time, it's more personal. I just wish I had more time to spend with her. There was some much I needed to apologize for. Why does the Lord always take the good ones away and leave people like me around?

"I can't answer for the Lord, but I can tell you to what he tells us in his word. Romans chapter 8 verse 10 reads, ***"And if Christ be in you, the body is dead because of sin; but the spirit is life because of righteousness."*** This body is not built to last forever, but the building of our faith ensures us of life beyond what this world can ever offer. Kelly faith gives little question where her eternal life will be. Now what you have to do is make sure your days are spent getting your life to line up with the word of God."

"Normally I would have a sarcastic response to what you say. This time, I can only agree. Thank you, sweetheart."

"It feels good to hear those words. Let's get some sleep, we have a long day tomorrow."

*********************

The morning had come faster than expected, but this has to be taken care of. I went into the bathroom allowing her to sleep a little longer. When I came out, she was just turning over.

"Good morning. How did you sleep?" I asked.

"Last night was peaceful for some reason. Usually, I toss and turn all night. I see you started getting ready. Give me about an hour and I will be ready."

"Take your time and we will leave when you are done. I'll go down and make us some breakfast." I replied.

While she gathered her things and went into the bathroom, I went down to the kitchen. Just as I about to start cooking, the house phone started ringing.

"Good morning, God loves you and so do I," I answered.

"Good morning Pastor Walker, this is Deacon Mosely. I wasn't sure what it is that you needed me to do doing the service."

"Morning Deacon Mosley. For now, I just want you and your family to be in the service. You can sit up front in your usual seat with the other church leaders. I will be giving the eulogy myself. We will see you in a few hours, and don't think I forgot about you telling me what was bothering you yesterday."

"Yes sir, I'll see you then. Give our best to First Lady," He said before hanging up.

I went back to preparing breakfast before Kerry was done getting ready. Afterwards, we shared a few hours in morning worship. We then made sure we had everything before heading over to the church. We didn't say too much because she was getting emotional with each mile we drove. I just pray she can hold it together enough to get through the service.

When we pulled up to the church, the parking lot was packed. Good thing I have a designated parking space. I looked over to check on Kerry, but she was already caught up entirely in her feelings. I parked and went around to help her out of the car. We went straight to my office from there. After getting her seated on the sofa, I had one of the mothers come stay with her. I went up to see how things were coming along.

"Good afternoon Pastor, How is the First Lady doing?"

"She is doing excellent Mother Mary. Thank you for asking. Also thank you for getting all the other mothers here today."

"You know we would never let you go through this alone, but I feel in my spirit there is more going on here than meets the eye."

"All in good time Mother. Now if you could tell the usher's to please get everyone seated. I'll go down and bring up the First Lady."

I tell you what, that Mother Mary is something special. I went back to my office to get my Bible and Kerry. There is never a good time to start a service like this, but waiting only prolongs the healing process.

"Honey, everyone is about here. We need to head up now."

"I can't believe that she is gone. Why did the Lord take my cousin?" She cried out.

I walked over, taking her in my arms trying to give her some comfort. Once she pulled herself together, we made our way into the hallway. From there, I had one of the Mothers help get her the rest of the way. I went straight up to the pulpit to get the service started. I looked over the crowd checking to see who was here because this is not going to be an ordinary homegoing.

"I want to thank everyone for coming out this afternoon. We have gathered today in a show of support for my wife and your First Lady's family as they will be laying her cousin Kelly to rest. Kelly and her husband Rodney have been members of the church for years. As their Pastor, this is a day I never look forward to. As a Christian, we know from reading the word of God, we all must pass this way. The question is, how will each one of us come prepared to answer for the life we led? This is what I want to talk about if I can."

I waited for a few seconds to see how everyone would react. Of course, there were the usual whispers of conviction among the crowd. I tried not to look in Kerry direction, but I couldn't resist. She had that look of a deer caught in the headlights of an oncoming car. I then directed my attention over to where Frank and his family was sitting. They looked so good together. I'm so happy things are working out in his life. I can still see myself in him when I was that age. Of course without the criminal past.

"Let us pray. Father, we come before you, asking that you give us peace that surpasses all understanding. We have come to many homegoing services, but still we find it hard to let go of our loved ones. We have been taught, that to be absent from the body, is to be present with the Lord. Father send your Holly Spirit to each member of the family. Allowing them to come to terms with your decision to call Sister Kelly home. We know your choices may be confusing to the unsaved, but to those of us who are called by your name, we receive your judgment. Today Father, give me a word for your people and myself. I decrease that you may increase. In Jesus name, I pray, and all Gods people said, Amen and Amen."

After I was done praying, the Holy Spirit came rushing over me like a flood. All I could say was "Yes Lord." What it told me, was total confirmation to what I was feeling in my heart.

"Deacon Mosley, could you please join me please," I said.

I waited until he made his way up to the pulpit. "I know this is a home going service for our Sister Kelly, but how many know that whenever something dies, something is born," I addressed the crowd as he was coming. Again I waited for the reaction from the people.

"People of God and friends of the family, I need your full attention, please. We will be moving along with the service, and I will be giving the eulogy. But, before that happens, I want to address you all first. I have been your Pastor for years and come to love you all. The last few years have brought so much to this church and my own personal life. The full revelation of what I tried to keep hidden has made me choose what is important in my life. I loved the Lord with all my heart and soul. This you already know. What has to be made clear now is how much I love my Wife. That is why this next statement is so easy for me. I will be stepping down as your Pastor, and in my place will be a man we have all come to love and trust. He doesn't come without his fair share of trials and tribulations. The Bible says in the book of Jeremiah, 3:15, *"And I will give you pastors according to mine heart, which shall feed you with knowledge and understanding."* With that being said, let me introduce your new pastor. Pastor Frank Mosley."

As I waited for him to step to the microphone, I watched as people started talking amongst themselves.

"People of God, please settle down. You maybe be asking why I am doing this now at someone's homegoing service. My answer to this is, as we lay Sister Kelly to rest, we will be laying to rest everything that has brought so much unrest to this great house of God. This church will move into a new direction with a fresh anointing of the Lord. I brought this church as far as I could bring it. When it starts to become more of me then the Lord, it's passed time to step down. Just as Sister Kelly's body had to do when cancer took more control then she could handle. She knew that her earthly body was not her source, but the salvation that came with the promise of eternal life was. Yes, she wanted to stay as long as she could because of the love she had for her husband and family. We knew as the cancer had spread to more of her vital organs, it took more chemo to keep it under control. When the chemo couldn't keep cancer at bay, the body started to shut down.

See that is what happens to each one of us living out of the will of God. We go through life doing our own thing hoping we never get caught. We live with the false sense of security that Grace and Mercy will cover our wicked sins. It says in the book of Hebrews chapter 10, verse 26, *"For if we sin willfully after that we have received the knowledge of the truth, there remaineth no more sacrifice for sins,"*

Grace and Mercy will only cover you as long as you stay within the words written in this Bible." I held my Bible up and walked to both sides of the altar. I wanted everyone to see what I meant.

"Once you choose to go your own way, don't expect the Lord to bless your mess. Yes, I said mess because that is what you will make of your life. The sad part is, you don't even consider the lives you impact along the way. You think because you are blessed, that you are in the will of the Lord. The Bible teaches us that the devil can give you gifts as well. The things of this earth are all not of God. It says in Matthew 6:19-21, *" Lay not up for yourselves treasures upon earth, where moth and rust doth corrupt, and where thieves break through and steal: But lay up for yourselves treasures in heaven, where neither moth nor rust doth corrupt, and where thieves do not*

***break through nor steal: For where your
treasure is, there will your heart be also."***

"See Sister Kelly, did not lay up anything
but her love for her husband, Brother Rodney,
family and the Lord. She kept no secrets that
will tarnish her legacy. Can each of you say the
same about your life? Before you answer,
remember that there is nothing you do that is
hidden from your Heavenly Father. The blessing
in all this, is that Kelly was right with the Lord
of Lord and King of Kings. She left this world
entirely at peace with her life. If she had any
regrets, it would be that everyone she wanted to
see saved and in the grace of God was not. If you
want to honor her legacy, then look deep into
your heart. If there is anything outside the will
of the Lord then let it be laid to rest doing this
home going service. This is your opportunity to
come back home to the Lord. This will be the
last altar call I do, and I would love to see Kelly's
vision come to pass. Will there be one who will
hear her message and come back home."

I waited for a few minutes to see if anyone came down. Just when I was about to speak, people all over the church started to stand where they were seated. Slowly they begin to make their way down to the front. They were coming from every direction. I couldn't do anything but start to cry because of the mighty move of God. Families were coming holding hands, men were coming with tears in their eyes, young ladies were coming while pulling down their little dresses.

"Look at God!" I yelled out. Even though it took someone passing away to get people to change, her life was not in vain. After all, Jesus died on the cross for all of us.

"Come home to the Lord people of God. the saved as well as the unsaved, you are invited. The heavens are indeed rejoicing as they welcome home Sister Kelly. Please move close as you can to make room for everyone. While people are still coming, I will make my way down to the floor. Pastor Mosley, this is where you come in. You will lead us all back to the Lord, and yes I said we. I count myself among the number here today. Please don't second guess the will of the Lord, remember you said yes a few years ago."

# Frank

I walked up to the pulpit after Pastor Walker handed me the microphone. My mind was spinning in every direction. Who would have seen this coming? Tears started running down my face as I fixed my mouth to speak. Who would have ever guess that the Lord would choose the likes of me to preach his word? Now he has placed me in the position of being a pastor.

I looked over to where Stacy was sitting, and saw she was completely in tears herself. This is a home going service, but also a homecoming service at the same time. I even noticed that Kerry was caught up in her feelings also. I looked towards the back of the church, it was like I saw my mother standing there with a smile on her face. Just then I heard the voice of the Holy Spirit whisper in my ear, "The Lord is well pleased with you." I knew right then I had to step into my calling.

"People of God, let us pray. Father God, you are a loving and forgiving God. You are the Alpha and the Omega. We come to you confessing we have fallen short of your will. We ask for your forgiveness and pray that the sins we committed have not caused you to erase our names out of the book of life. Father, we know that we abuse the Grace and Mercy that you extend us daily. This is why we are here to repent. I will give one last call to anyone who has not yet come down to the alter. The Lord will forgive and welcome you back into his loving arms. Come now why the blood is still warm in your veins."

Just as I was about to come down and pray for the people gathered, Kerry stood up and starting walking to where Pastor Walker was standing. From the other side of the room, Stacy was coming holding Gabby in her arms. "God is so good!" I shouted out loud. I started laying hands on each person and saying a short prayer over them. When I came to Kerry, she was still crying with her arms straight in the air.

I reached over placing one hand on her shoulder. "Sister Kerry, are you here to recommit your life back to the Lord?" I asked.

"Yes, yes, Lord please forgive me for being a sinner. I caused so much pain and hurt to so many. I was hurting so I didn't care for anyone but myself," She cried out.

"Sister Kerry, the Lord has heard your plea and has already forgiven you. He has been waiting with open arms to welcome you back home. The Holy Spirit has spoken to me and told me of the hurt you and Kelly had to endure as children. The Lord said you have been carrying this burden for too long, and it's time to let it go. Sister Kelly is at peace and gone on to be with the Lord. Now it's your turn to be at peace. The Lord has seen fit to allow you to remain among the living because your purpose has not been fulfilled. He wants to take all your sins and throw them into the sea of forgetfulness. He told me to tell you, cry today because tomorrow, it's time to get back to living."

"Yes Lord, I hear you and I will obey. Thank you, Pastor Mosley, for being a faithful friend. I'm ready to come back home to the Lord," She replied.

"Do you repent of all your sins and accept Jesus Christ as your Lord and Savior?"

"Yes, with all my heart, and I do this in loving memory of my cousin Kelly," She replied.

"Then welcome home Sister Kerry. Welcome home where you belong."

I left her in the arms of Pastor and made my way over to where Stacy was standing. She also was still in tears. I had one of the Deacons hold Gabby before I began to pray with her.

"Can you tell us why you made the decision to come down today?"

"I'm tired of living the life I been living. I want to know the Lord for myself. That could easy have been me lying in that coffin. I don't wish to leave this earth without being saved. I want to be a good Mother, Wife, and Fist Lady of this Church."

"Do you believe that Jesus Christ is the Son of God and that he died on the cross?"

"yes, I do," she replied.

"Do you repent of your sins and accept him as your Lord and Savior?"

"Yes, I repent and welcome him into my life!" She shouted out loud.

"Then welcome home my Sister and my soon to be First Lady of Road to Redemption Church of God."

I tried to hold back my emotions, but they took over away. I reached over taking Gabby into my arms as she even was in tears. I handed the microphone back over to Pastor Walker so he could pray for us as a family.

"Father, I come before you asking that you will bless this family as they move forward on their new journey. I pray that no lack will ever come into their lives and that blessings will always overtake them. May their hearts always be focused on you, and their lives be a testament to your word. Father, I ordain him this day as the new pastor of Road to Redemption Church of God. With you in the mist, this church will always be in great hands. In Jesus name, Amen."

When he was done, I went back to praying for everyone else. When that was done, we moved to the cemetery to complete the service. We may have buried Sister Kelly, but in the process, we brought so many people back to the Lord. This has truly been a day in the will of God. My family has been made hold, Kerry has been restored not only to God but to herself, my transformation is now complete. Undercover Deacon has become a permanent soldier for the Lord.

The End

CPSIA information can be obtained at www.ICGtesting.com
Printed in the USA
LVOW10s0907030416

481969LV00019B/683/P

9 781523 484812